B[illegible]

HUW COLLINGBOURNE

dark neon

ISBN: 978-1-913132-20-0
Published by: **dark neon**

http://www.darkneon.com/

Also by Huw Collingbourne

Cold War Thrillers

(Kennick)

Kill Job

The Exodus Plague

(Post-apocalyptic)

Book 1: The Snow

Book 2: Imprisoned

Book 3: Escape

Book 4: Saturday Night In The City Of The Dead (*stories*)

The 1980s Murder Mysteries

(Comedy crime capers)

Book 1: Killers In Mascara

Book 2: The Glam Assassin

Book 3: Death Wears Sequins

TABLE OF CONTENTS

This pamphlet is about a small group of people who have accepted thermonuclear war as a probability, and are consciously and carefully planning for it.

They are above the Army, the Police, the Ministries or Civil Defence. They are based in fourteen secret headquarters, each ruled by a Regional Commissioner with absolute power over millions of people. In the whole of Britain only about 5000 men and women are involved; these chosen few are our shadow military government…

They are quietly waiting for the day the bomb drops, for that will be the day they take over…

(From the document, "DANGER! OFFICIAL SECRET" published by the Spies For Peace, 1963)

1. After The Bomb

"Good afternoon," she said. "Are you dead or dying?"

She was a sandy-haired girl, early twenties, wearing a white nurse's uniform and a British Army issue metal helmet.

"I don't think I'm either," I said.

"Oh!" She smiled. "Then you must be walking wounded. If you go over to the marquee, you can get a cup of tea and a fairy cake."

The marquee was a big red-and-white-striped tent that had been erected on a patch of scrubby wasteland just beyond a ruined house. The street down which I was walking was a scene of utter desolation: there were houses with roofs and walls missing; smoke and dust was drifting through the air; the stink of burning rubber came from a smouldering armchair squatting next to the scorched remains of an old mattress.

Hackney was not looking at its best that day. Bodies lay all over the place. As I stepped over a pile of rubble I happened to bump into a middle-aged woman with a nasty head wound who appeared to be trapped beneath a fallen beam of wood. I tried to imagine where the beam had come from, out in the middle of the High Street, but my imagination wasn't up to the task.

"'Ere, watch what you're doing!" the woman with the head wound shrieked at me. "You nearly trod on me arm."

"I'm sorry."

"It's broken, you know," she said proudly. "In two places."

"That must be painful," I said.

She laughed. "Oh, I don't mind. Last time it was me legs that was broke. Had to be carried orf in a stretcher. The stretcher-bearers nearly dropped me. I don't mind a broken arm so much 'cos I'll be able to walk on me own two feet as soon as someone gets this telegraph pole off me."

The beam of wood was a telegraph pole then. That possibility hadn't occurred to me.

"Good luck!" I said.

I was in the process of stepping gingerly over a tangled mess of iron girders beneath which a child's teddy bear was trapped (a poignant touch, I thought) when my attention was attracted by a pompous little voice which, I soon saw, belonged to a pompous little man.

"Just a moment! Just a moment! What do you think you are doing?"

The man clambered over the iron girders, callously treading on the teddy bear as he did so. He was a short, plump man wearing a dark uniform that looked like a well-pressed boiler-suit and a black pie-dish metal hat on the front of which was written, in white paint, "W", which identified him as a warden.

"I was on my way to the marquee," I said.

"The marquee! The marquee! What's your name?"

I told him. He was carrying a large notebook. He flipped through its pages ostentatiously, tutting to himself as he did so. "There's no Kennick listed here," he said at last. "If you are not in my book, you shouldn't be here."

"And yet," I said, "I am."

His moustache bristled and his eyes glared fiercely from behind his little round, wire-framed glasses. "Why are you going to the marquee?" From the superior tone of his voice, he seemed to think he had trapped me with a question which I could not answer without incriminating myself.

"I was on my way to get a cup of tea."

"Tea!" he spluttered with a tone of such outrage that he made it sound as though I had confessed to selling orphaned children into slavery.

"And a fairy cake," I added.

From the purple colour that was suffusing his face, I worried for a moment that I might have gone too far. Perhaps the shock of my dissolute cravings for tea and fairy cakes would prove too great for his constitution to withstand.

Then a cultured voice oozed into the air from just behind my shoulder. "It's quite all right, Featherglade." (Featherglade, I gathered, was the warden's name) "Mr Kennick is our guest. The Ministry sent him."

The speaker was a tall, grey-haired gentleman wearing a dark, pinstriped suit. Although he wore civilian clothes, it was obvious that he was a military man. He had the bearing, the authority and the mad gleam in his eye that told you he was used to giving orders and having them obeyed.

"Major Willoughby-Styrt, sir, I didn't see you there." Featherglade snapped the heels of his shoes together in the Prussian manner and was half-way to giving a salute but then thought better of it and stroked his moustache instead. "The Ministry, eh? Yes, well, I rather thought that must be the case." Featherglade's hitherto pompous demeanour changed in an instant. The purple colour left his face, the pursed lips and frowning brows which had been aimed in my direction moments earlier vanished like summer clouds before a breeze, to be replaced with a sunny smile that looked as though it had accidentally strayed onto the wrong face. "Yes well, I hope you didn't mind my checking your credentials, Mr Kennick. One must observe the correct protocols, you know. No fear or favour here."

"I'll look after Mr Kennick now, Featherglade," the Major said. "How are the levels holding up?"

Warden Featherglade was holding some sort of contraption, about the size of a paperback book in his hands. The contraption had a dial on it, like the speedometer of a car. Looking at the dial, Featherglade said, "Averaging three roentgens per hour at the moment, sir. Another twenty minutes and we'll need a change of personnel."

"Good work, Featherglade. See to it."

"Mind yourselves!" a braying voice called out behind me as two uniformed Army men rushed past carrying a stretcher upon which, casually smoking a cigarette, reclined the woman who had formerly been trapped beneath the telegraph pole. Apparently, her lack of broken legs didn't excuse her the indignity of being stretchered away after all.

"Another survivor, Corporal Welbridge?" the Major bellowed jovially.

"Oh, yes, sir," the leading stretcher-bearer called back. "Me and Taffy," (he nodded towards the second stretcher bearer) "got a score of fifteen injured and two dead so far."

"Jolly good! Jolly good!" replied the Major.

Corporal Welbridge and Taffy trotted off rapidly in the direction of a waiting ambulance while the smoking woman on the stretcher waved at me.

"Good man, that Welbridge," said the Major enigmatically. "I wish they were all like him." For a moment, his thoughts seemed to be elsewhere. Then, snapping back to the business at hand, he turned to me and said, "I'm afraid, it's all a bit chaotic here, Mr Kennick. But, you see, I thought it might help you to understand something of what we are up against."

"Preparations for Armageddon, by the looks of things, Major."

"Ha! Yes! Well, we have to get everyone trained, do you see, to deal with the worst, should that ever be necessary. Oh, and don't bother with the Major malarkey. I'm a civilian now, after all. People like Featherglade will insist on using my Army rank. But, frankly, I think we should be on first name terms, don't you. Please call me Edward. And you are…?"

I don't make a habit of getting on first name terms with clients. "Kennick," I said.

"Ah. Yes, well, quite."

"How many people are there in this operation?" I asked.

Looking around at the soldiers, the wardens, the medics and nurses, the ambulance drivers and the firemen – not to mention the dead and the wounded lying on the ground or staggering about amongst the rubble – I guessed that there must be a couple of hundred people in all. My guess was wrong.

"There are about a thousand men and women involved in total. Though, if you will forgive me, I must correct your terminology. This is not an operation, you see. It's an exercise. There is a difference, you know. This one's called Civil Defence Exercise Sandcastle. Don't ask me why it's called Sandcastle. For all I know, someone in the Home Office flips through a dictionary and picks the first word they put their finger on. We have these exercises fairly frequently. But Sandcastle is one of the bigger ones. Of course, not all the people involved are on site at the moment. Some of the victims have been driven away already. And most of the chaps who did the makeup left this morning."

"Makeup?" I said.

"Well, you didn't think all these wounds and radiation burns were real, did you? Though, I must admit, some of them are damned convincing."

We were, at that moment, walking past the burnt-out wreck of a small, four-seater car in the front seat of which sat a wretched man, his face smeared with grime and his long overcoat charred, presumably by the heat of a nuclear blast. Throwing himself into the spirit of the thing, the man groaned at us most movingly.

"What's going on over there?" I pointed towards a crumbling redbrick building that had been reduced to little more than a rectangle of ruined walls with neither window-glass nor roof in sight. A rescue team on the upper floor of the building was in the process of lowering a body on a stretcher using an ad hoc and perilous-looking pulley contraption made from ropes and metal poles.

"Ah yes, well, you see, we may have to rescue people from all manner of different locations. This building has three storeys. But others might have six or ten. We must be prepared for all eventualities."

The descending stretcher suddenly gave a lurch. One end began to descend considerably more rapidly than the other end. The victim, who had been firmly secured to the stretcher using buckled straps, let rip with a series of profanities which showed that, while the bomb had not finished him off, he was concerned that the rescue team might. After a few moments, the pulley ropes were adjusted and the victim was lowered to the ground with a bump that occasioned another volley of profanities.

"They mean well," said the Major with a tone more of optimism than conviction.

"Stand aside! Stand aside!" a raucous voice cried as a speeding stretcher went past, this one bearing a horrifically burned teenager who, showing commendable resilience in the face of adversity, put up two fingers and blew a raspberry at us.

"I think perhaps," said the Major, "we might go somewhere a little less frenzied, don't you? To discuss the nature of our little problem without being subjected to quite so many distractions."

"I was on my way to the marquee," I said. "I am led to believe that refreshments are available."

"Ha! Stewed tea and rubbery custard slices are about the best you can expect there. It is my opinion that if the Soviets don't kill us with their bombs, the Women's Institute will see us off with their tea and cakes."

On the way to the marquee, some people started shouting at us. I can't recall exactly what they were shouting but the general idea seemed to be that they didn't think much of us and they hoped we'd die a long and painful death. When I turned to see who they were, I noticed a small crowd – a dozen people or so, I suppose – standing behind the chain-link fence which surrounded the ruined town in an attempt to prevent unauthorised access. The people on the other side of the fence were carrying placards bearing such uplifting slogans as "They Live! We Die!" and "Nobody Will Survive".

"What's all that about?" I asked.

"Peace protestors," the Major replied gloomily. "Damned bloody layabouts, more like. Got nothing better to do with their time."

2. Chalk And Toilet Rolls

"Oh, it's you again!" It was the sandy-haired nurse whom I'd met earlier. She was sitting alone at a table just inside the marquee. "Craving for a cuppa, I expect."

I noticed the thick, scummy brown liquid which she was drinking from a mug. "Not 'craving', exactly," I said. "No beer, I suppose?"

"Funny you should mention that," said the Major. "I have a couple of bottles of Indian Pale Ale put away in a secure location."

"Hello, Teddy!" The nurse addressed the Major with a breezy informality. "I hope you hid the beer well. They're a light-fingered bunch, these Women's Institute people."

The Major smiled and pointed to the chestnut leather briefcase he was holding. "Never let the important stuff out of my hands."

"Good idea!" the nurse said, chuckling.

The marquee was surprisingly busy. People with suppurating wounds and bandaged heads sat around at tables, chatting, laughing, smoking cigarettes, eating sandwiches and generally having a jolly good time. Considering that London had just been destroyed by one or more H-bombs, they seemed to be doing remarkably well at keeping their spirits up.

"If you don't mind my asking," I said, "what's the point of all this? If the Soviets drop the bomb, there won't be enough of London left to worry about, will there?"

The Major gave me a disapproving look. "Oh, we must look on the bright side, Mr Kennick. Assuming a ground-burst ten megaton bomb, the major area of immediate destruction would be confined within a radius of, say, five or six miles."

I didn't know much about H-Bombs so I believed him. I have a trusting nature. It's one of my biggest faults. "So Hackney should get off pretty lightly, then." I tried to put a smile into my voice.

"As long as we are properly prepared, we shall make a much better job of things than the cynics and the peace protestors would have you believe."

"And that's what *this* is all about? Preparing people?"

"Training. The general public may not be aware of quite how well prepared we are. Indeed, it would be true to say that we are prepared for any eventuality. We're all working together, you see. The Army, the Air Force, the Civil Defence Corps..."

"The Government?"

"Well, yes, the Government, naturally. However, that is something I am not entirely at liberty to discuss. But I can assure you that the public at large would be astounded if they knew of our level of preparedness."

A woman suddenly laughed raucously at the table next to ours. Glancing across, I noticed that the woman's face was so badly burned that much of the skin was peeling away. Next to her sat an older woman whose face was covered in wounds and whose ragged grey pullover was stiff with congealed blood. The injuries evidently gave the two women not the slightest discomfort.

"We have almost three hundred casualties, you know," the Major said proudly.

"Impressive," I said. I nearly added, "I'm sure the sight of all these plucky Londoners with their fake wounds and their tea and fairy cakes will give Mr Brezhnev a few sleepless nights," but I decided against it since the Major had given no signs of possessing even a rudimentary sense of humour.

At the centre of the marquee there was a table covered in a red chequered cloth upon which stood mounded plates of desiccated cakes and curling sandwiches. Two formidable looking women with steel grey hair and a military bearing dispensed the provender with rigorous fairness. Each casualty was allotted two sandwiches, a cake and a mug of tea. If anyone attempted to take more than their fair share, one of the women would inform them of the error of their ways in a booming voice that would put most Sergeant-Majors to shame.

On seeing the Major, the nearest steel-grey woman smiled ingratiatingly and extolled the merits of the congealing tea which she was dispensing from the tap of a large chromium-plated urn. Ignoring her blandishments, the Major took two half-pint glasses (he shook his head curtly when the woman asked him if he'd like some milk in those) and headed briskly towards a table at the remote end of the marquee.

Once seated, the Major took from his briefcase two bottles of Indian Pale Ale, a bottle-opener and a sheaf of mimeographed paper. Having opened the bottles, poured out the beer and passed one glass to me, he peeled off the top sheet of mimeographed paper.

"There. What d'you make of that?"

I drank some of the beer. It was warm and slightly flat. I glanced at the sheet of paper. Then I glanced at the Major. My first thought was that this was some sort of practical joke but the Major's expression told me that he wasn't the sort of person who went in for jokes. My second thought was that he'd given me the wrong piece of paper.

"What is this?" I said.

"What does look like? It's an inventory."

Typed on the sheet of paper was a long list:

"Gummed labels (plain) – 100,000
Toilet rolls – 12,000
Pencils (HB) – 700
Boxes of chalk (white, 144 sticks per box) – 25
Erasers (pencil) – 1,000
Ball-point pens (black) – 10,000
Rubber bands (assorted) – 100,000"

...and so on.

"Are you saying someone's stolen all this?"

The Major looked at me as though I was a fool. I tried not to take offence. There are some people in the world who look at everyone as though they are fools and I had the feeling that the Major was one of them. He picked up his glass of beer, held it up to the wan light filtering through the red-and-white-striped fabric of the marquee, swirled it, sniffed it, took a good long swig, put it down on the table, fixed me with a gimlet eye, and said, "I am told that you are trustworthy, Mr Kennick."

"That's nice to know." I was wondering to myself who'd told him that. "I was recommended to you, then?"

"In a way."

"Do you mind if I ask, by whom?"

He raised his eyebrows. Both of them. It's something that people of his class do quite a bit. They generally do it when they are talking to people of my class. I don't know if they do it deliberately or if it's something they can't help doing when they are forced into contact with inferior forms of life.

"Just an acquaintance," he said at last.

I tried to imagine which acquaintance of his might also be an acquaintance of mine. It might have been one of my former clients but I doubted it. The people I work for generally come from what are known these days as "the lower middle classes". In other words, they are working class people with cocktail cabinets. I didn't think the Major would be likely to mix in that social milieu. Which just left some of what you might call my "professional" contacts. People I do certain special jobs for, from time to time, whether I want to or not.

"Have you heard of Turnstile?" the Major asked.

I gave him a blank look.

"How about Subterfuge?"

I laughed. "It's what I do for a living."

"Stockwell?"

"I know Stockwell," I said. "Not far from Clapham."

He shook his head. "Then how about Burlington?"

"Are we going to play a game of 'What's My Line'? Or are you going to tell me what you are talking about?"

"Suffice it to say, Mr Kennick, that there are elements of Civil Defence which I am not at liberty to discuss. Turnstile is one such element."

"So why mention it?"

"I was told that you are a competent investigator. As such, I presume that you may be able to discover more than Her Majesty's Government would wish me to reveal. What I can tell you is that certain documents may have fallen into the hands of persons whose interests are inimical to the security of our country."

I handed back the sheet of mimeographed paper. "This shopping list of gummed labels, boxes of chalk and toilet rolls?"

"Precisely."

"You think the KGB is interested in our toilet rolls?"

"The list of items which I have shown you is one of the less sensitive documents. I don't suppose you've signed the Official Secrets Act, by any chance?"

"If I had, I wouldn't be at liberty to tell you."

He smiled. Maybe he did have a sense of humour after all. But it was buried so deep that it rarely saw the light of day. "Very good, Mr Kennick. Most droll. I shall interpret your answer in the negative."

"Would I be right to assume that whoever filched your missing documents didn't sign the Official Secrets Act either?"

"That I cannot tell you. Principally because I do not know the identity of the person who, as you say, 'filched' the documents."

I had a bad feeling about this. From what I could gather Major Willoughby-Styrt was something mid-ranking in the Civil Service, attached in some capacity to the Home Office. This wouldn't be the first time Home Office documents had got themselves lost. I didn't know what was the usual procedure for investigating the loss of secret documents but I was fairly sure that it was not normal practice to engage the services of a suburban private investigator whose day-to-day work rarely involved anything more exciting than finding stolen cars and missing teenagers.

"The person who recommended me to you," I said. "You wouldn't care to tell me who that was, I suppose?"

I don't know if he had any intention of answering my question because in the next moment our discussion was interrupted by a penetrating scream. The Major, being a man of a quick intelligence, looked at me and said, "Is that someone screaming?"

I told him that it sounded very much as though it was.

"That's not permitted, you know," he informed me. "It could be mistaken for the real thing, you see. I shall have to go and check. Just in case..."

3. The Body In The Sweetshop

We left the marquee. The organised chaos which I had seen earlier had now been replaced by disorganised chaos. People in Army uniform were running around shouting at people who were not in Army uniform. The dead and dying were rising *en masse* from the rubble and standing around gawking. Someone was blowing a whistle, someone else was telling people to stand well back; an elderly man in a dusty pin-striped suit was claiming to be a doctor and demanding to be let through while a plump woman with a fake head-wound had just stopped screaming and was now babbling hysterically at anyone who would listen that it was "horrible, horrible it was, found him I did, lying there, blood everywhere, never in all my days ain't I seen nothing so horrible!"

"It's Welbridge, sir." What with all the noise and confusion, the man's voice could barely be heard. It was the officious little warden, Mr Featherglade, the man who had tried to intimidate me with his notebook in whose hallowed pages my name did not appear.

"Taffy found him, sir. Private Evans, that is. In the sweetshop. Having found him, Taffy called me. And, having been called, I blew my whistle." He held up his whistle as though it were a sacred artefact. "Blowing the whistle is specified in the book. The book for wardens, sir. So, in the manner specified, I blew my whistle and…"

"For God's sake, shut up, man!" The Major pushed past Warden Featherglade, then he pushed past the hysterical woman; he pushed past the gawking crowd of onlookers and finally he arrived in the doorway of a wrecked, roofless building over the broken window of which hung a flaking sign stating: "Thomas and Sons, Sweets and Tobacco".

As the Major cut a swath through the spectators, I followed in his wake until I found myself in a position where I could see the body lying amidst the rubble inside the building. It was a man's body in uniform. The old man in the pin-striped suit, who had announced himself as a doctor, was already leaving the building and walking towards the Major. His face was grim and he was shaking his head.

"Better call it off for today," the doctor said.

Already some soldiers were trying to push back the crowd of watchers.

"Dead?" said the Major, in a tone of voice that suggested it was a damned bad show for a soldier to die without prior authorisation.

"Afraid so," said the doctor.

I noticed then that that the nurse I'd spoken to earlier was kneeling next to a soldier who was sitting on a pile of bricks just to the left of the sweetshop. The soldier was crying and the nurse was talking to him in a low voice. I guessed the soldier must have been the man they called Taffy, who had found the body of Corporal Welbridge.

"He shouldn't have been in the sweetshop in the first place!" That was the annoying little warden again. He had pushed his way through the crowd and was now addressing the Major in the sort of condescending tone that bank managers (in my experience) reserve for people who have wilfully exceeded their overdraft. "I told him. I told them all. 'Stick to the locations authorised,' I said, 'and by no means enter buildings without authority.' If he hadn't been in the building this would never have…"

The Major turned to me. "It's those damned peace people."

I wasn't sure I'd heard him correctly. There was a lot of noise, due to all the people talking and shouting and calling for order; and, on top of that, there were the sirens of police cars and ambulances arriving. I asked the Major to repeat what he'd said.

"Those damned peace people. CND. Ban-the-bomb. Whatever they call themselves. They'll be behind this, mark my words. I've been trying to warn our chaps for years but I was never listened to."

I thought of mentioning the fact that the peace demonstration was located outside the perimeter fence whereas the body of Corporal Welbridge was located inside the perimeter fence. But I kept the thought to myself. I assumed that an ex-British Army officer working in a position of responsibility for the Home Office would be capable of making this important observation for himself. Besides which, nobody was paying me to investigate the death of Corporal Welbridge so it was none of my business.

Well, it wasn't at the time.

4. A Hot Day In The Office

It was Monday morning and too hot to move. A fly was buzzing around the office but I couldn't be bothered to swat it. When the phone rang, I couldn't be bothered to answer it.

"You want me to answer that?" Meek had his feet up on my desk. His feet were next to the phone.

"Might as well," I said. "Could be a client."

I hadn't had a client for over two weeks. Normally, I'd have been eager for the work. But I'd done a biggish sort of job a few weeks earlier and I was still living off the proceeds. Meek had been living off the proceeds too, albeit in an unofficial capacity. He hung around the office and scrounged off me: cups of tea, digestive biscuits, on one memorable occasion half a bacon sandwich.

Meek picked up the phone. "Kennick Investigations. Can I be of assistance?"

There was a pause while someone told Meek in no uncertain terms that he could not be of assistance. Meek grimaced and made a two-finger gesture into the air. The fly gave an apathetic buzz.

"It's for you."

I was sitting at the other end of the desk with Straker curled up in my lap. Straker is my cat. I reached over to take the phone from Meek. The movement disturbed Straker. He showed his displeasure by digging his claws into a part of my anatomy into which, as a general rule, I do not like to have claws dug. I groaned into the phone.

"Is that you, Kennick? Are you drunk?"

I knew the voice. It was a voice I did not much care to hear. It belonged to a man called Becker. The last time I'd heard that voice, trouble had followed. Trouble is something I try to avoid. Then again, money had followed the trouble, so every cloud has a silver lining.

"Drunk?" I was offended by the accusation. "Me? Drunk? Two cups of cold tea and a glass of warm water is all that's passed my lips."

"You were groaning."

"An old war wound."

"I thought you worked alone. Who was it who answered the phone?"

"An old friend of yours. Meek."

Meek glanced across at me. He didn't like being talked about unless he knew who was doing the talking and what was being said. There were people who had grudges against Meek and some of those people didn't mind how they went about settling them. If someone with a grudge managed to track him down, it was Meek's ambition to be somewhere else. I don't think Becker settles grudges in that way. Then again, I can't be sure. I lay back in my chair. The cat didn't like that. He dug in his claws and I groaned.

"You're groaning again," Becker said. "Are you sure there isn't something wrong with you?"

"Thanks for the concern, Becker. Did you call to enquire about my health or was there some other reason?"

"We have a job for you."

"I think you've got the wrong end of the stick. I'm not doing any jobs for your lot. Not now. Not ever. Those kinds of jobs are bad for my health. These days I just handle ordinary, everyday sorts of jobs. Divorces, runaway kids…"

"…shop assistants who embezzle the cash," Becker chipped in. "Yes, I've heard your patter before, Kennick. From your lack of clientele, I'd say you either ought to get yourself a new business or get yourself some new patter."

"Oh, very funny, Becker. You should go on the stage. You'd have them rolling in the aisles. Anyway, it was lovely to hear your voice again but, as I was saying, I'm not interested in…"

"How can I put this politely, Kennick? The thing is, this is not a request. It is a requirement."

"Don't make me laugh!" I laughed, just to drive home the point. "I'm my own boss these days, Becker. I don't take orders from anyone. Especially not from you."

"They are not my orders, Kennick. They come from rather higher up the ladder, one might say."

"Like who? Her Majesty?"

Becker chuckled. Or, to be more accurate, he made a kind of strangulated choking noise which is the closest Becker ever gets to chuckling. "I am not at liberty to provide you with any more details than I already have. But it's really quite simple. We should like you to keep an eye on a certain individual of interest to us."

"Keep an eye? That's it?"

"That is, as you say, it. Actually, it should all be very easy. It should, in fact, involve no work at all."

"You'll pay me for doing no work at all? You think I was born yesterday?"

"It's true. I promise you. You see, all we want you to do is keep an eye on a certain person on whom you will already be keeping an eye."

I tried to think who Becker was talking about. I glanced at Meek. He was watching the fly buzzing around the edge of his coffee cup. I don't have a wide social circle. Meek is the only person I see on a more or less regular basis and that's only because he keeps dropping around uninvited.

"Any clues as to who this person might be?" I said into the phone.

"I thought you'd have guessed."

"I don't like guessing. Just tell me."

When I put the phone down, three things happened in quick succession: first Meek hit his coffee cup with a rolled-up newspaper; then the cup fell onto the floor and the handle broke off; and finally Straker dug his claws deep into my thighs, made a wailing noise, leapt off my lap onto the floor and then leapt into Meek's lap. Meek groaned as the claws went in.

"What did you do that for?" I said.

"The cat dug his claws in," he replied.

"I wasn't asking why you groaned. I was more curious to know why you knocked your coffee onto the floor."

"I was swatting the fly."

Since the fly was still buzzing around above my head, I assumed that the swat had been unsuccessful.

"I'll deduct the cost of that cup from your salary."

"You don't pay me a salary," Meek reminded me.

I was trying to think of something scathing to say but my thoughts were interrupted by an arthritic little tinkle from the bell over the front door. When I glanced across, I saw a young woman walking into the office. She was a petite brunette with the sort of hourglass figure that's supposed to have gone out of fashion. Meek has never followed fashion much; he sat up in his chair, arranged some papers and pencils on the desk as though he owned the place, flashed as much of a smile as his nicotine-stained teeth were capable of flashing and said "Can I help you, miss?"

"Are you Mr Kennick?" she said, her dark brown eyes flicking nervously between me and Meek.

"Well, I'm…"

I interrupted. "I'm Kennick."

"Oh, I…." she glanced at Meek again. "It's a bit delicate, you see. I was hoping to, you know…"

"It's something you'd prefer to discuss in private?" I asked.

"Well, yes, I suppose it is."

"My colleague was just leaving." I rummaged in my pocket and pushed some coins across the desk towards Meek. "Go and get yourself a cup of tea. Ask for an unbreakable cup."

"You can speak in front of me, miss." Meek flashed his yellowing teeth again. "I'm very discreet." The young woman did not seem impressed.

"And bring back the change," I told Meek as he reluctantly left the office.

"See you later, darling." He winked at her. She did not reply. I formed the opinion that she was a person of good taste. The bell tinkled again as the door closed.

"Take a seat," I said. "No need to be nervous. I'm like a priest. I hear everyone's problems and I never talk about them."

"I'm not religious." She took a seat. "It's a personal matter."

I smiled. It was not the sort of smile that Meek had flashed at her – two acres of teeth and eyes out on stalks. Mine was a sympathetic smile tinged with what I hoped looked like a world-weary sadness. "Would you like something to drink?" I said. "Tea? Coffee? Um… water?"

Straker was winding himself in and out of the woman's legs with his tail in the air.

"I love cats," the woman said. She scratched Straker behind an ear and he made a purring noise. "Is this your cat?"

"He adopted me. Now, why don't you tell me what the problem is, Miss…?"

"Honeyfield. I mean Brigg. Mrs Kitty Brigg. Honeyfield was my maiden name."

I took out a pad of lined paper and a Biro from my desk drawer and wrote her name on the first line. Kitty Brigg made a little gasping "Oh!" sound when I did that. I looked up at her.

"Sorry," I said, "is anything the matter?"

"I didn't know you'd have to write anything down. I mean, I don't want him to know I've been to see you."

"Him," I thought. So that was it. "Your husband?" I asked.

She said nothing for a few moments then she gave a little nod and said "Mmmm."

She was blushing slightly. That told me everything I needed to know. "You think he's been playing around?" I suggested.

She sighed, almost deflated. I hoped she wasn't about to cry. But she just looked at me and said, "How much do you charge?"

5. The Art Of Detection

"So what's her problem?"

Meek and I had gone down the local pub, The King Harry, after I'd shut up the office for the day. We were sitting at a table in the corner, right under a moth-eaten stuffed hog's head that glares balefully through glass eyes from its commanding position on the wall.

"The usual problem," I said. "Her husband's seeing another woman."

"What a berk! He must need his eyes tested." Meek's always had a keen eye for women. The trouble with Meek is that where his eye goes first, his hands are all too likely to follow. Which is why I'd sent him out to get a cup of tea. I'd given him half a crown and I was still waiting for the change. I knew I'd never get it. I'd trust Meek with my life but I don't trust him with the petty cash.

"Blimey!" Meek continued, "a geezer's married to a bird with a figure like Jayne Mansfield, and he's still not satisfied?"

"Some men are greedy," I said.

Meek warmed to the theme. "I mean, most men, if they had a bird like that, they wouldn't have the time to go after other birds, would they? Nor the energy, neither. If you know what I mean…"

"I think I get the general idea."

"How old is she? Can't be much more than nineteen."

"Twenty-three," I said. "The husband's twenty-four. They've been married for two years. No kids. Pleasant little semi-detached house in a leafy suburban street. Willow Street. About ten minutes' walk from here."

"That must have cost a few bob. Where did the money come from?"

"Not from Mrs Brigg. She works in a newspaper shop. Her husband, however, is an accountant."

"Dodgy lot, accountants. No wonder he's got plenty of dosh."

"And that's another funny thing. He's got more dosh now than he should have."

"Dipping his fingers in the petty cash?"

"He bought himself a fancy new watch. Bought a twin-tub washing machine and a new cooker for the missus."

"Not the romantic sort then?" Meek sniggered. "You want to keep a woman happy, you buy her perfume and chocolates."

"Maybe he's buying perfumes and chocolates for other women?"

"He's probably one of these gigolo types. Can't keep their hands off anything in a skirt."

"You'd know about that, I suppose?"

Meek smirked. "So who's her hubby bonking, then? Has he got a special bird or is he playing the field?"

"That's the mystery. She doesn't know. All she knows is that he goes out two nights a week. On his own. Regular as clockwork. Up to town. Catches the tube. Mondays and Thursdays. Started about four months ago."

"Today's Monday," Meek said. This was a fact of which I was already aware so I did not gasp with astonishment. "Shouldn't you be...?"

"Following him? Nah. Too soon. For one thing, I don't even know what he looks like. For another thing, I haven't been paid. Mrs Brigg is going to call in to see me again, tomorrow." Meek gave me a suggestive wink which I pretended not to notice. "She's bringing a photo. Of her husband. And an advance payment."

"What's he get up to on Mondays and Thursdays, then?"

"He claims he's taken up with some peace people. The ban-the-bomb lot. Says he goes to meetings."

"But his missus has her suspicions?" Meek took a long slurp of beer to give him time to mull over the possibilities. "Been coming home with lipstick on his collar, I expect."

"Not at all. He comes home with ban-the-bomb leaflets."

"The cunning bastard."

"Of course, he might be telling the truth."

"What? About going to ban-the-bomb meetings? Nah. The ban-the-bomb mob never wash and they've all got beards." Meek took a drag on his cigarette. "And that's just the birds."

"Has anyone ever told you you're uncouth, Meek?"

"All the time. You want me to follow the geezer? Find out what he's really up to?"

"I'll follow him," I said. "By a lucky coincidence, I'm not doing anything special on Thursday evening."

"I was thinking…" Meek said.

I suppressed the urge to make a witty comment.

"What I was thinking was, if you want to grow your business, you need to get more detectives. Well, one more detective anyway. Namely, me."

Meek had done a bit of work for me once or twice before. He kept trying to get me to employ him on a permanent basis. But there wasn't enough work to keep me fully occupied as it was. I didn't need a full-time assistant. I told him so.

"You don't have to pay me," he said. "Not while I'm learning the ropes, anyway. 'Course, once I've learnt the ropes I'll no doubt be able to bring in more business, so that would change things, I suppose."

"I suppose it would," I agreed. "But it's more complicated than that. You don't just get up one day and suddenly you're a detective. You have to learn the art."

This is true. I'd learnt the art from a chap called Roddie Glenster. He was one of the old-time detectives. Tough as nails and wouldn't take no for an answer. I did eighteen months with his agency. I signed up for two years but I got six months remission for good behaviour.

"I can learn," Meek insisted. "I'm fed up of drifting from one lousy job to another. I want something, well, solid. I mean, it seems to me there must be more to life than just, you know…"

"Sex and violence?" I suggested.

"Living a carefree existence," Meek said. "There comes a time in a man's life when he has to make a choice between living for himself or, you know…"

"Dedicating himself to the betterment of humanity?" I was joking but Meek didn't notice.

"Spot on!" he said. "The betterment of humanity. Well, I am now at that time. In life. Me. Now."

"And that's why you want to be a detective?"

"Exactly. I mean, I've got the experience, ain't I. Working in security and that..."

The sort of security Meek worked in involved chucking drunks out of late night boozing clubs and putting the boot into shop-owners who'd forgotten to pay protection money to Soho thugs. Meek was muscle for hire. He had never been too fussy about who did the hiring.

"There are all kinds of skills you have to learn," I said.

"Yeah? So how do I get started?"

I smiled. I wasn't taking him seriously. My mistake. "You start by memorising car numberplates."

He winked at me. "Yeah, yeah, yeah."

"That's how you start," I said. "If you want to be a private investigator, you have to train your memory. Memory and observation, those are the two principal qualities of a good detective. Whenever you come into the office from now on, memorise the numberplates of six cars parked in the street. Then, when you sit at your desk, write down what you remembered and then go outside and compare the list you've written with the numberplates of the cars in the street."

There is a trick to remembering numberplates but I'd forgotten what it was. To be honest, I've never found any use for memorising car numberplates. All I know is that it's something that trainee private investigators are expected to be able to do. If only I could have remembered the trick, I'd have told Meek what it was. But since I'd forgotten, he'd just have to figure it out for himself. He looked crestfallen. "Trouble is," he said, "I've never been good with numbers."

I sighed, indicating that this might be an insurmountable barrier on the road to a career in the private investigating business. Then Meek's expression suddenly brightened. "I'm pretty nifty with my fists, though. That's got to be useful, ain't it?"

"I haven't got any use for fists just at the moment. Following a bloke who's having a bit on the side without his wife's approval is not a job that's likely to involve a great deal of pugilism."

"You got this other job, though," Meek went on. "The one you're doing for Becker..."

I shrugged. "I haven't agreed to take that on."

"What was he after, anyway?"

"It doesn't matter. I wasn't interested."

"Oh?" Meek didn't try to hide his disappointment. In fact, he glared into his empty beer glass then he glared at me. I got the impression it was my turn to buy the next round. I went to the bar and got two pints plus a whisky chaser for Meek. The whisky chaser raised his spirits.

"There is another job though," I said.

"Yeah? Which is?"

I hadn't told Meek about the malarkey I'd been to the previous day. I told him now. I gave him a brief outline of the job I was doing for the Major but I didn't go into details, mainly because I didn't have any details to go into. Something had been stolen. A list of office supplies and toilet rolls, as far as I could tell. So what? Meek didn't seem interested. Then I told him about Civil Defence Exercise Sandcastle.

"Civil Defence!" He took a drag on his cigarette and blew smoke out through his nostrils to show his contempt. "Cor deary me! Civil bleedin' Defence! Waste of bleedin' time that is! What was they doing? Running around with cardboard guns shouting 'Put that light out'?"

"Not exactly." I gave Meek a short summary of Exercise Sandcastle. I told him about Bully Fen, which is the part of Hackney where the Army goes to play its war games. I described the streets filled with ruined buildings, the dead and the dying with their simulated wounds, burns and broken limbs; I told him about the wardens and the soldiers, the stretcher-bearers and the rescue teams. I didn't mention the pretty nurse as I didn't want him to get side-tracked.

"Sounds like a lot of weekend bleedin' do-gooders," was Meek's reaction. "People pretending to be dead! What a load of bollocks. I bet they'd faint if they saw a real dead body. "

"As a matter of fact, they didn't."

"Who didn't?" said Meek. "What you on about? Who didn't do what?"

"Nobody fainted when they saw a dead body. Someone screamed. A few people looked a bit grey around the gills. But no one fainted."

"Yeah, but that's what I was saying. They was only playing dead. Which is not the same as being dead, is it?"

"They weren't all playing."

I told Meek about the body of Corporal Welbridge which had been found in the bombed-out sweetshop.

"Bloody Hell!" he said. "So now you're investigating a murder?"

"Nope. For one thing, I've no reason to suppose it was a murder. For another thing, it's got nothing to do with me."

Meek guffawed. Which made the cigarette smoke go down the wrong way and he spent the next minute choking and coughing. When he'd got his breath back, he drank down the rest of his beer and said, "'Course it's got something to bleedin' do with you! I bet that's why Becker phoned you, wasn't it."

I shook my head. "That's where you are wrong."

Meek wasn't wrong, as it turned out. But I didn't know it at the time.

6. A Rainy Night In Kilburn

On Thursday night, it rained. It didn't just rain, it poured. It not only poured, it also thundered. If there's one thing I can't stand, it's thunder. Don't ask me why. I'm not easily rattled. At various times I've been punched, stabbed and shot at. While it is true that I don't like being punched, stabbed and shot at, I don't lose sleep worrying about it. Thunder, on the other hand, brings me out in a cold sweat. Or, on this occasion, a hot sweat. It was an oppressive, muggy night and I was standing in a doorway in North London somewhere around Kilburn way. The sweat was running slowly off my forehead into my eyes before gathering speed as it headed south. It was the sort of night when I'd have liked to have been inside an air-conditioned bar drinking a lager straight from the fridge. On a warm night, there's nothing to beat an ice-cold Tiger beer. I got a taste for Tiger beer in another place and another time, years ago and far to the east of Kilburn.

The reason I was standing in a doorway in a street in Kilburn was that the doorway happened to be directly opposite a certain decrepit old building that I was keeping a close eye on. The building looked as though it dated from Victorian times and hadn't aged well. Kitty Brigg had told me that it was to this building that her husband went on Monday and Thursday evenings. Or, at any rate, he'd gone there the previous Thursday and, unless he was doing a tour of the clapped-out Victorian buildings of London, it seemed a reasonable bet that he might come to the same building this Thursday. It wasn't hard to find. Mrs Brigg knew exactly where it was and how to get there due to the fact that she'd been there herself. She'd followed her husband the previous Thursday. According to Mr Brigg, an organisation called "The International Peace Collective (North London Branch)" held meetings there.

Now, maybe you are wondering why Mrs Brigg was paying me to track her husband's movements when she'd already tracked them herself. All I can say is, that's the way things often happen with infidelity jobs. It's been my experience that when a woman decides her husband is having an affair, she doesn't wait quietly at home while he goes off philandering. She follows him. By the time she gets around to hiring an investigator, the chances are she knows everything there is to know – his mistress's name, her age, where she lives, her favourite perfume; maybe even the colour of her underwear. Mrs Brigg hadn't got quite that far. But she had found the building he'd gone to. She had even had a look inside. She had followed her husband up to the first floor and along a corridor. She had watched him go into Room 2B. At which point Mrs Brigg had scarpered. She had come to the conclusion that following her husband into the rookeries of darkest Kilburn was a job best left to a professional. Which explains why I was now lurking in a doorway watching the place.

It was one of those buildings that was so ugly you couldn't help but wonder why anyone had built it. Three storeys high, it had six windows on each floor. I tried to figure out how many rooms there were inside. Assuming each room had two windows, there would be nine rooms in total. However, the building was on the corner of a street and an alleyway and I had only counted the windows on the side facing the street. I took a look down the alleyway. There were another six windows per floor on that side of the building. Which meant there were thirty-six windows in total. So, if there were two windows per room, that meant there must be eighteen rooms in the building. Unless, of course, the corner windows in the alley opened into the same rooms as the corner windows on the street? Then again, maybe each room had only one window? Or maybe some rooms had three windows? Or even four? And maybe there were rooms with no windows at all?

You don't have to tell me, because I already know, that trying to figure out the number of rooms in a building by counting the windows is a pretty damn' pointless activity. It was doubly pointless because I didn't even care how many rooms there were. The number of rooms was not germane to my investigation. Then again, look at it from my point of view. I was standing in a doorway at night in a seedy side-street in one of the more depressing parts of Kilburn, I'd been standing there for over an hour, and I had nothing to think about except the rain and the windows. So I thought about the windows.

When you are on a job you have to think about something or you'll go nuts.

There were only two lights on in the entire building: one on the ground floor, one on the first floor. The top floor was in darkness. I'm guessing that once upon a time, back when Queen Victoria was a girl, it may have been a residential building, but not any longer. The rooms had been converted into offices for businesses that couldn't afford one of the concrete and plate-glass monstrosities that are popping up in the more salubrious parts of town.

Mr Brigg – whose name, I now knew was Frank but he preferred to be called Frankie – had gone into the building in Kilburn at around half-past eight. He came out again at twenty-five past nine. I recognised him thanks to some photos that his wife had given me. When Frankie Brigg went into the building, he'd been alone. When he came out, he had company. A woman. About his age, I'd say – early twenties – but there the similarity ended. Frankie Brigg was conventional to the point of old-fashioned. He was wearing a cheap-looking gabardine raincoat over a single-breasted dark suit. On his head was a battered trilby hat. He wore the sort of glasses favoured by the television comedian, Harry Worth: big frames with a severe straight edge across the top. His clothes, his glasses and his manner all made him look middle-aged. Yet I knew for a fact that he was twenty-four.

The girl he was with, on the other hand, was definitely one of the swinging set: black miniskirt, thigh-length white vinyl boots, long blond hair, transparent plastic mac decorated with abstract swirls of colour. If he was The Establishment, she was The Alternative Society. They made an odd pair but they seemed to be getting on all right. When he opened up his umbrella, she snuggled up closer to him and, as they set off up the street away from me, I could hear her laughing. Frankie Brigg doesn't look the sort to crack jokes. Then again, neither does Harry Worth.

I was just about to follow them when two men came out of the building. One of them gave the impression of being part of the "with it" set – a tall, willowy chap with long, unkempt hair and a string of beads around his neck; he was dressed in a knee-length coat with a fringe of fur that looked as though it had been eaten by some exceptionally undiscerning moths; he had a sharp, beaky nose and protruding teeth. The other one – who was a shortish, muscly sort of chap, conservatively dressed in a dark-blue, single-breasted suit – reminded me of Mick McManus the all-in wrestler.

Having stepped out of the front door, the two men had a quick gawk at the rain which was unrelenting, and then decided to stay in the shelter of the porch for a couple of minutes while they finished their cigarettes. Since they were stationed there, right across the street from where I was standing, I couldn't go haring off after Frankie Brigg and the girl because Mick McManus and his friend with the teeth would be sure to see me. Having seen me, they might take it into their heads to wonder what I was up to. With most people, most of the time, I wouldn't have been bothered what they'd thought I was up to; but there was something about those two that made me think they were worth being bothered about. I got the feeling it wouldn't be good for my health to bring myself to their attention. If the worst came to the worst, I could probably deal with the taller one but I wouldn't like to go hand to hand with his thuggish-looking friend. So I waited in the shadows and I tried to hear what they were talking about, just in case it had any bearing on the job I was working on, but what with them being on the other side of the road and what with the noise of the rain pelting down, I couldn't hear a thing.

Eventually, when they'd they finished smoking their cigarettes, they turned up their collars, pulled down the brims of their hats and set off down a side street at a fairly brisk pace. I didn't have any reason to follow them and, by that time, I didn't have any hope of finding Frankie Brigg and the blonde girl so I decided to make the best of a bad job and have a poke around inside the building that I'd been watching for the last hour.

7. Room 2B

"Can I help you, mate?"

He was young (mid-twenties, I'd say), slim, rather a flashy dresser: pale cream turtle-neck sweater, dark blue slacks, collar-length auburn hair. I'd walked up the staircase to the first floor and was making my way down the corridor, doing my best not to drip too much over the worn black-and-white tiled linoleum, when this chap had surged out of a room and confronted me in a surly manner as though I might be a common crook or a down-and-out looking for a spare broom cupboard to have a kip in. It is not my habit to make myself known to people I might want to keep an eye on, so I was none too pleased to see him. But what with the corridor being lit by a bare 40-watt bulb and what with the brim of my hat turned down and the collar of my coat turned up, I was hoping he wouldn't have a chance to get a good look at me.

"I was looking for someone," I said.

"Who?"

"Well, I…" I couldn't think of anything clever to say but I needn't have worried because the flashy chap interrupted me before I had a chance to say anything:

"What's the name of the person you are looking for?"

I had to think fast. I'm not at my best when I think fast. I said, "Mr Worth." It was the first name that came into my head because I'd been thinking of Harry Worth a few minutes earlier. It could have been worse. I could have said I was looking for Mick McManus. In which case, he may have spotted my deception.

"Not here, chum," he said.

"This building is number 47, isn't it?"

"Fifty-seven," he said. "You've got the wrong place, chum."

That was the full extent of our conversation. I mumbled something and he went back into the room. There was a brass plate next to the door. It said: "2B. Baron's Fine Living". There was no mention of "The International Peace Collective (North London Branch)". Maybe they were a secret society? I didn't know who or what Baron was but if his idea of "fine living" was a run-down room in a squalid building at the wrong end of Kilburn, I guessed they probably didn't do much catering to the aristocracy. It occurred to me that I might have come to the wrong place. Maybe Frankie Brigg hadn't gone into room 2B after all. I only had his wife's word for that and I wasn't convinced that she was a reliable observer. Mind you, since there were only two rooms with lights on in the entire building, he must have gone either into 2B or into the room on the ground floor.

I trotted down the stairs. The corridor on the ground floor was just as shabby as the corridor on the first floor. I walked along to the room that had a light on. Even though the door was solid wood, I could tell there was a light on because there was a half-inch gap at the bottom of it. The sign next to the door said: "1B. Irena Duvere (appointments only)". I was left wondering what Irena Duvere's line of business might be. She could have been anything from a chiropodist to a ballet instructor. My familiarity with the seamier side of London life also suggested another possibility which I am too much of a gentleman to mention. But whatever she did was her business and not mine so I turned up my collar and headed towards the outer door.

For all I knew, Irena Duvere might have been the femme fatale responsible for leading Mr Brigg astray. My intuition, however, told me that this was not likely. What's more, my intuition also told me that the two men I'd seen standing in the porch – the tall man with the teeth and the muscly one who looked like Mick McManus – were more likely to have some connection with the flashy dresser on the first floor than with Irena Duvere on the ground floor. Which meant that all three of them had something to do with Frankie Brigg and the blonde girl who'd left with him. My intuition also told me that they didn't seem like the sort of people who would be likely to spend much time trying to work out how to ban the bomb and bring about world peace. If you'd asked me to take a guess at what sort of people these were, I'd have guessed villains. The bloke who looked like Mick McManus was your average East End heavy – useful with his hands, not so useful with his brains. The tall man with the teeth was a hanger-on. Not a serious crook, just a grifter. The flashy-dresser who'd spoken to me in the corridor though? I wasn't so sure about him. He could have been anything from a glamour photographer to a pimp. But that wasn't my business. My business was tailing Frankie Brigg and finding out if he was sowing his wild oats where they shouldn't be sown. Too late now. I'd lost him. I'd have to follow him some other night. If he went off with the blonde girl again maybe I'd have a chance of finding out where they went and what they got up to.

There was no point hanging around in Kilburn any longer so I pulled my coat lapels tight around me, ducked my head against the rain and headed towards the nearest tube station. As I walked up the street I happened to glance at number 47 which was the address I'd told the flashy dresser that I'd been looking for. It turned out that number 47 was a ladies' lingerie shop. I couldn't help wondering if he'd known that all along, in which case he might have assumed that I have what is known in the trade as "specialist interests"; or else he had clocked the fact that I wasn't being straight with him. In which case, he might have wondered what I was up to. In which case, he might decide to ask around to see if anyone knew who I was. In which case, if he really was a villain, I'd have to be careful not to get on the wrong side of him. But no, I told myself, a fashionable bloke like that wouldn't be bright enough to get one over on an old hand like me. I was wrong. He was a lot brighter than I gave him credit for. And a lot more dangerous. But I'll get around to that later.

8. An Unexpected Visit

Friday morning was nothing to write home about. I walked from my flat to my office, which took me all of ten minutes. I tried to think what I would do with the day. My investigation into Major Edward Willoughby-Styrt's stolen documents was as dead as the proverbial dodo. This was mainly due to the fact that I didn't know what of any significance had been stolen, who had stolen it or what the Major expected me to do about it. When I had asked him for more details he'd given me the whole spiel about how it was all very hush-hush, my dear chap, and he was not at liberty to say anything to the likes of me since I hadn't gone to the right school, don't you know. In other words, I'd been given the brush-off. Someone higher up had instructed him to cooperate with me but he intended to make his cooperation as limited as he possibly could. All I had to go on were some names that I didn't understand, like clues from a cryptic crossword puzzle: Burlington, Stockwell, Turnstile, Subterfuge.

My time would probably be better spent working on the infidelity job. But what could I do about that on a Friday morning? Frankie Brigg would be at work so, in all probability, he wouldn't be doing much in the way of infidelity. Which meant that I was at a loose end. I bought a newspaper. I decided to spend the morning with feet up on my desk, doing the crossword.

When I opened up the office, Straker, my cat, was standing outside the front door waiting for me to let him in. Once inside, I put the kettle on to make some tea and gave Straker a saucer of milk. He lapped it up, then settled down and went to sleep on Meek's chair; or, at least, on the chair in which Meek would have been sitting if Meek had been there at the time, which he wasn't. Meek's like that. Some days he turns up, other days he doesn't.

I spent the rest of the morning doing the crossword and then I went down the King Harry for lunch. I had a half of shandy, which warm and flat, and a plate of stale shepherd's pie which tasted of stale shepherd. On the way back, I popped into the chemist's and bought a packet of Rennie's tablets because I had a premonition that I was about to suffer from a bad attack of indigestion.

I was sucking a Rennie when I went into the office and found Meek with his feet up on my desk. Standing on the desk, right next to his feet, was a little china ornament, about ten inches high. It was a rosy-cheeked girl wearing a flouncy frock and a flouncy hat and she was holding a lamb in her arms. The lamb reminded me of the shepherd's pie that I was trying hard to forget.

"What's that?" I said.

"What?" said Meek.

"That horrible little statuette standing next to your horrible big feet."

"Oh, that!" said he. "I got it down the Lane." By which he meant the market in Petticoat Lane. Meek conducts certain business arrangements down there. I don't ask for the details. I'd rather not know. "What d'you reckon it cost me?"

I looked at him, amazed. "You *bought* it?"

"Go on," he said, "guess how much it cost."

"Fifty quid," I said, just to pull his leg because I wouldn't have given you threepence for it. But he took me seriously and I saw a gloating expression on his face.

"Ten bob!" he said. "Well, ten and six."

"They saw you coming!"

"The thing is," he said, "these little trinkets go for a fortune down the Burlington Arcade."

"Do they?" I wasn't really interested. I loosened my tie, put my jacket over the back of my chair, grabbed the electric kettle which was standing on the draining board of my sink and started filling it with water. "Burlington Arcade," I muttered to myself. "Burlington, Stockwell, Turnstile. I wonder how many Burlingtons there are in London? Burlington Arcade, Burlington House, Burlington Gardens..."

The subject didn't grab Meek's attention. "Here," he said, and he threw a small writing pad at me which very nearly made me drop the kettle. Somehow I managed to catch the pad in my left hand as I was plugging the kettle in with my right hand. Then I stared at the pad. It was covered in pencil scrawl. It looked like a code of some kind. A jumble of numbers and letters.

"What's this?" I said.

"I been doing what you told me."

"Which is?"

"Car numberplates. You said I should memorise numberplates from six cars parked outside. Well, there they are."

"Well done. How many did you get right?"

"Don't know. I haven't checked."

"Well, then. You better check, hadn't you."

I threw the pad back to him but my aim wasn't great. The pad bumped into the hideous statuette and nearly knocked it off the desk. I've never seen Meek move so fast. He lunged towards the toppling figurine and caught it before it had a chance to hit the floor and put its miserable existence to a timely end.

"Strooth!" he said. "That was close."

"I don't know what you're so bothered about," I said. "You can get better tat than that from Woolworths for under a bob."

"Ha! Shows how much you know," said Meek. "This here is genuine Meissen."

"Oh, yeah?"

"Yeah. That's exactly what it is."

I tried not to laugh but I didn't succeed. When I finally managed to stifle my hilarity, I told him, "That thing you've got there is plaster of Paris, which is a fancy way of saying it's made of chalk. Go down the fairground in Brighton and find yourself one of those stalls where you win prizes by chucking ping-pong balls into goldfish bowls. Usually you can either win a teddy bear, an ornament or a goldfish. The ornaments are just like the one you've got in your sweaty paws. Shelves full of them they've got in Brighton Fun Fair, all waiting to be won."

"Nah," he said. "What do you know about it anyway?"

"What I know," I told him, "is that if I was ever able to get a ball into one of them bowls, I'd tell them I'd take the goldfish. Where's Straker?"

Talking about fish had reminded me of the cat. Sometimes I get him a tin of sardines. He prefers them to cat food.

"Went out when I came in."

I should never have given Meek a spare key. He came and went as though he owned the place. Just like the cat which, at that very moment, was mewing at the front door, waiting to be let in. I let him in.

"There's the cat," said Meek, stating the bleeding obvious.

I began to wonder what to do with the rest of the day. The options that presented themselves were: feeding the cat, swatting the fly which seemed to have taken up permanent residence, or talking to Meek. I fed the cat, I couldn't be bothered swatting the fly and there was nothing on God's earth that I wanted to talk about with Meek. So I sat in the chair behind my desk and tried to look busy.

"I'll be off then," Meek said eventually.

The kettle started to whistle. I looked up from my notepad. I'd been making notes relating to the infidelity job. There weren't many notes to make so I'd started drawing cats in the margin of the paper. "I was just about to make tea," I said, and carried on scribbling cats. I didn't want Meek to think I wasn't rushed off my feet.

"Yeah, well, I don't think I'm in the mood for tea," said Meek.

"No?"

"I'll be off then."

"Right. You better check the numberplates. On the cars. The ones you memorised."

"Yeah, good idea. See you tomorrow, then."

"Tomorrow's Saturday."

"Is it? Oh, I'll see you Monday then."

I got up and turned off the kettle.

The bell on the door tinkled as Meek left. I breathed a sigh of relief. I then opened the window, loosened my tie, put a couple of spoonfuls of tea into the cracked, brown teapot that I keep poised at the ready on the windowsill, then poured the hot water from the kettle into the pot. It was like old times. Just me and the cat and a relaxing mug of tea. It was too good to last. No sooner had I poured the water from the kettle into the pot than the bell over the door tinkled again. I turned around, expecting to see Meek. I thought he must have had a change of mind and decided to spend the afternoon lounging around my office doing nothing after all. At that moment, there were few people I wanted to see less than Meek. But this was one of them.

"What the...?"

"Please, no vulgar language, Mr Kennick. I bring glad tidings. Oh, you are making tea, I see. A small cup would be most agreeable."

It was a man I'd had dealings with before. His name was Turlough McJay and he was a shortcut to trouble.

9. A Message From A Friend

My office is not made for comfort. It is what I like to call "Spartanly furnished". I have a desk, three chairs (only one of which has a cushion), a paraffin heater, an Imperial 66 typewriter (for typing up reports and invoices), a small grey metal filing cabinet, a sink, an electric kettle with a whistle, and a calendar which shows a scenic view of Morecambe Bay. I also have an ashtray advertising Watneys Red Barrel. Meek gave it to me. I don't know where he got it. I didn't ask him. Turlough McJay was sitting in the chair with a cushion. He was depositing the ash from an evil-smelling cheroot, which is a sort of inadequate cigar with delusions of grandeur, into my Watneys Red Barrel ashtray.

"I thought you'd moved on," I said.

"I beg your pardon? Moved on?"

"To another department."

McJay blew out a stream of stinking smoke. "You make it sound as though I work in a gentleman's outfitters, Mr Kennick. That is not quite how our – what shall I call it? – it is not the way our enterprise operates."

"Well, you know, it's always a pleasure to see you," I said through gritted teeth, "but, as you can no doubt see, I'm busy. Rushed off my feet. I have a business to run. As it happens, business is booming at the moment."

"Mr Becker told me you were rather abrupt."

"Was I? When was this?"

"When he telephoned your office. On Monday, I am given to understand."

"Was it as long ago as that? How time flies."

"It seems he did not have the opportunity to describe to you the nature of the job which…"

"Ah, now there you've put your finger on it, Mr McJay. Jobs. I'm overwhelmed with jobs. Which is why I haven't got the time to take on new clients."

"But we are not new clients, are we? Besides, no additional effort is required from you. You are already working for Major Willoughby-Styrt."

"I may be. Or I may not be. Client confidentiality forbids me to reveal anything about who I may or may not be working for."

"All we wish you to do is to tell us the same things that you tell him. Embellished, perhaps, with a few other details, should they happen to be of interest."

"I'm a suburban private investigator, McJay. Not a double agent. You and the Soviets may have spies that work for *them* and spies that work for *you*, and half the time the spies that work for *you* are the same spies that are working for *them*. That's not how I work. The way I work is, someone comes to my office, they have a problem they want me to solve, they pay me to solve it. Once I get my grubby hands on their money I do what they want me to do. I don't double-cross them. I don't spy on them."

"Aha!" Turlough McJay's self-satisfied expression became even more self-satisfied. "I see you are labouring under a delusion, old boy."

"I am, am I? And what delusion would that be?"

"You appear to think that Major Willoughby-Styrt has commissioned you to undertake some work on his behalf."

Turlough McJay has one of those unctuous voices that sounds like cream in the process of curdling. The man suits the voice. He favours tweed jackets that must have cost a packet once upon a time but which have gone downhill ever since. The expression on his face looks permanently amused in a slightly seedy way as though he's just worked out the punchline to a blue joke. He stinks of cheap cigars and whisky. For some reason that I can't quite put my finger on, I don't entirely trust him.

"Major Willoughby-Styrt phoned me," I said. "I met him. He gave me a down payment in the form of three used fivers and a ten-bob note. If that's a delusion, I could do with more of them."

McJay grinned and snorted. "Ha! Ha! Yes, I see what you mean, dear chap."

"Look, McJay. I am not your dear chap, or your old boy and I will not discuss work that I am doing for a client. So, if you have something to say, say it. Otherwise, well… I have other things to get on with."

He stubbed out his cheroot in my Watneys Red Barrel ashtray and blew the last of the foetid smoke in my direction. "The thing is, dear fellow, the, er, 'three used fivers and a ten bob note' with which Major Willoughby-Styrt paid you…"

I put up my hands, palms facing towards him, to show that I had come to the end of my tether. "I told you, I won't discuss a client's business. If that's all you have to say then…"

"It's not his," McJay interjected.

"What isn't? What are you on about?"

"The money. The fifteen pounds and ten shillings. It was not withdrawn from Major Willoughby-Styrt's personal bank account."

"I don't care where the money comes from."

"As far as the Major is concerned, the payment for your services is not a personal expense but a business one."

"So what?"

"As you are no doubt aware, Major Willoughby-Styrt works for the Home Office. Perhaps you are labouring under the delusion that it is the Home Office which is paying to engage your services? With all due respect, Mr Kennick, the Home Office is not in the habit of engaging the services of, well – how might I phrase this? – a not entirely successful suburban private detective."

That thought had already occurred to me but I didn't want to add to McJay's sense of self-satisfaction by telling him so.

"The fact of the matter, Mr Kennick, is that someone of our mutual acquaintance was informed of the little problem besetting the Major and it was he who recommended that the Major seek out your services."

"The Old Man?" I said.

"I beg your…?"

"The mutual acquaintance who recommended me. I'm assuming it was the Old Man. The head of your very secretive department."

"The identity of the individual is quite irrelevant."

"Not to me, it isn't."

"What I am trying to convey to you, Mr Kennick is that, we are your clients. It is we who are paying for your services. We are just as keen as Major Willoughby-Styrt to find the miscreants responsible for abstracting certain documents and to deal with them as appropriate."

I didn't care for the sound of that "deal with them". There are certain special sorts of jobs that call for certain special sorts of skills. The KGB, which has a nice way with words, call them "wet jobs"; they have a division, Department 13, which specialises in them. The British security services are more coy. Officially they don't do them. Officially, unlike the Russians, they have no department of "wet affairs". But unofficially there are times when people have to be got rid of. Naturally, our security services can't soil their hands with that sort of thing. Not directly. But still the jobs need to be done – quickly, efficiently and discreetly.

Not everyone can do that sort of job. Killing is easy. You get a gun, you pull the trigger and *bam!* the target falls to the ground like a duck in a shooting gallery. But guns attract attention. But, for this sort of job, attention is the one thing that has to be avoided. Which means killing at close quarters. Plenty of people can kill at a distance. Not so many can do it when they are close enough to smell the other man's sweat and hear the grunt as the knife goes in. The only people I ever knew who could do that kind of job had a few screws loose. They took pleasure in it. Anyone who takes pleasure in a job like that is not someone you can trust.

And then there's me.

The thing is, I'm a peace-loving sort of chap. I help old ladies cross the street, I take care of stray cats and put ten bob notes into the Salvation Army collecting box. I'm so soft hearted that there are days when I can't even be bothered to swat a fly.

But when a job has to be done, I do it. I do it calmly, quickly and efficiently. Some jobs can only be done by a specialist. I'm that specialist.

"I'm not interested," I told McJay. "I did a job for you once before. Once is enough."

"Oh, come now, Mr Kennick. This matter is quite different. You are already conducting an investigation for Major Willoughby-Styrt. We happen to be financing that investigation. It seems to me entirely reasonable that you should keep us informed of its progress."

When he put it like that, I had to concede that he had a point. Even so, I didn't like the way I'd been set up. I didn't like the way I'd been tricked into working for them. If I'd known they were going to be paying my fee when the Major had first contacted me, I'd have turned down the job there and then. McJay knew that. Becker knew that. The whole damned organisation knew that. So they'd tricked me. I wasn't surprised. It's what they do best.

"All being well," McJay said, "your investigation should be quite undemanding."

"And all *not* being well?"

"You will be reimbursed for any additional work that might be necessary. In extremis, a small – or, perhaps, not so small – ex gratia payment will doubtless be made."

In extremis, ex gratia, he'd probably learnt the fancy words when he was at Eton, or Harrow, or borstal or wherever it was that he'd misspent his youth.

"If you want me to bump someone off," I said, "just tell me."

He chuckled. "As I said, Mr Kennick, I fully expect this little matter to proceed quite smoothly. It should be a piece of cake, as the saying goes."

I didn't believe that. I know the people who McJay works for. When they want a job done, you can bet you'll get your hands dirty. But there was no point in arguing. If I didn't do the job, they'd get someone else to do it instead.

"It's not the way I work," I said.

"Then you will have to change the way you work."

"And if I say no?"

"You won't."

"I do."

"Then you must change your mind."

"Or what?"

"I beg your pardon?"

"I know a threat when I hear one no matter how plummy the voice that makes it. If I don't change my mind, what will you do?"

"I won't do anything. No, my dear boy. Nothing at all. But I fear some other people may. Certain parties know certain things. About you. Certain things you have done that are, well, frankly, not fully in accordance with the laws of the land."

"If you try to take me down," I said, "I'll take you down with me. If the police start investigating me, the trail will lead back to you."

"The trail? How very melodramatic! There is no trail. There really is nothing at all to connect you to me. Or to… well, whomever else you might have had in mind."

"The things I've done. Things beyond the law. I've done them for your department."

"My department? You keep talking about my department. I really have no idea what you mean."

"You, Becker, the Old Man. The whole sordid lot of you in your nice clean offices in Whitehall, or wherever it is you are these days."

"You really don't understand, do you? I am naught but a messenger. I bring you a message from a mutual friend. Professionally, however, I am a perfumier."

I laughed so much I spat some tea onto my desk and had to mop it up with my handkerchief. "A what?"

"Here." He handed me a business card. It said "Turlough P. McJay. Senior Olfactory Compositor." And it gave an address in Covent Garden.

"That card's as fake as you are," I said.

He tutted. "But for the fact that I am aware of your dry sense of humour, I might easily be offended. So, I shall be pleased to be able to inform our mutual friend, I assume, that you will be more than happy to accept his proposition."

They had me in a vice. I knew they had and they knew they had. I did jobs for them and they paid me. They paid me well. I'd had enough. I didn't want to work for them again. But they had me trapped. If I got uppity and didn't do what they wanted me to, one day they'd decide I was more trouble than I was worth. If I became a problem to them, one day the job they'd want done might have my name on it.

"Who do I report to?" I said. "You or the Major?"

"Well, both of us, naturally. Though I must emphasise that in no circumstances should the Major be informed that you are reporting to us."

"Why not?"

"Come, come, Mr Kennick. We need this investigation to be conducted with the utmost discretion."

"You don't trust him?" I said. "You think Major Willoughby-Styrt is up to something? Selling Britain's toilet roll secrets to the KGB? Or the CIA?"

"Ha! You have such a vivid imagination! Major Willoughby-Styrt is, needless to say, unimpeachable. A man of unblemished integrity."

"So what do you want me to find out, exactly?"

"We wish you to discover who appropriated the documents. And why?"

"The first thing I'll have to do is go to the Major's office and have a good shufty," I said.

McJay looked horrified. "Oh no. That won't do at all."

"Why not?"

"Discretion, my dear chap. We can't have you searching through his drawers. It would invite comment."

"But if that's where the documents were stolen from…"

"We can't be certain of that, can we?"

"It's the best place to start," I said.

"You may observe the proceedings of his department from a distance," McJay said. "If you think that it is really necessary to do so. But I must insist that you act with the utmost tact."

With some reluctance, it seemed, to me, McJay gave me the address of the Major's offices in Whitehall. He also gave me the address of the Major's town house and his country house. From the address of his town house, it was obvious that the Major wasn't short of a few bob.

"I suggest that you speak to Major Willoughby-Styrt's assistant, Mr O'Donnell."

"Why to him?"

"It was Mr O'Donnell who noticed the absence of the documents."

"You think O'Donnell had something to do with it?"

"I have no thoughts at all on the matter. Then you should visit Major Willoughby-Styrt's house. By which I mean his country house. He has a cottage in a nice little village somewhere close to Watford.

He also has a flat in Chelsea. He frequently stays in the London flat during the week. But he invariably goes to the country cottage at weekends. He was at the cottage when the documents disappeared."

"Someone broke into his cottage? And yet he didn't notice that they'd been stolen until this man O'Donnell in London told him?"

"Ah no. It's a little more complicated than that. On the weekend when the documents were purloined, there was a village fair, or possibly a fête – at any rate, something involving cake competitions and tombolas – which took place on the Saturday. That was a couple of weeks ago, on the 16th of July. And there was also an ROC training event on the Sunday. The Royal Observer Corps. You are familiar with them?"

"The people who keep a lookout for Luftwaffe planes – Messerschmitts and Junkers? I shouldn't have thought there were many of those flying about in the skies over Watford these days."

"The ROC no longer watches for enemy aircraft. These days they watch for bombs. Thermonuclear bombs, for the most part."

"And have they spotted any?"

"Not as far as I am aware. At any rate, that is not relevant to your investigation. What is relevant is that, on the weekend when the documents were taken, the Major was involved in an ROC training event at some small distance from his home. It is something which you may wish to bear in mind."

"You want me to go there? To this place near Watford?"

"I should not like to dictate your methodology, my dear chap. But it is something which you might wish to consider."

"When?"

"Tomorrow. There is some sort of ROC event scheduled. I'm sure it will be most illuminating."

"You've got everything planned already, haven't you!"

He gave a condescending wave of his hand. "There is also, of course, the worrying little matter of the unexplained death."

I grunted. This was due to the fact that Straker had just leapt into my lap and had forgotten to sheathe his claws. McJay, however, assumed that the grunt was intended to indicate an ignorance of the unexplained death which he had mentioned.

"The death to which I allude," he said, "was that of the young man during the Civil Defence exercise in the Bully Fen district of Hackney. I was given to understand that you were present at the time."

"Very sad and all that," I said. "But it's got nothing to do with the job I'm doing for the Major."

"You think not?"

"The man might have had a heart attack. Or a brick might have fallen out of the wall and hit him on the head. Some of the buildings in that place are death traps. I'm surprised they don't have more accidents."

"Oh, but my dear fellow, it wasn't an accident. It was murder."

Now it was my turn to laugh. "Give over! There were hundreds of people there. It was broad daylight. How could he have been murdered?"

"With a Fairbairn-Sykes knife between the fourth and fifth ribs."

"You are joking!"

"I assure you that I am not. I have a copy of the pathologist's report in my office. To be perfectly frank with you, Mr Kennick, we are rather more interested in the death of Corporal Welbridge than we are with the Major's documents. Though, of course, the two events may not be entirely unconnected."

10. Double-Booked

It was the middle of the afternoon when the doorbell tinkled again. I was hard at work on the crossword. I slid the newspaper off the edge of the desk and onto my lap so that any prospective client who might have wandered in wouldn't get the wrong impression. I needn't have worried.

"What are you doing here again?"

It was Meek. "There's something about your magnetic personality that keeps drawing me back," he said. "Also, I came to get that."

I followed the direction of his glance. He was looking at the hideous statuette standing on my desk.

"You're welcome to it," I said.

I spread the newspaper out on my desktop and turned my attention to 7 Down: "Touchy feline reverses into old hat." Meek, meanwhile, took the opportunity to put on the kettle to make some tea. Then he sat down and told me one of his long, meandering stories about someone he'd met who'd said something funny and someone else he'd met who'd had a run-in with the law which, judging from the way Meek was chuckling, was also funny. I never bother listening to Meek's stories. They are usually about people I don't know and don't want to know and they are never as funny as Meek thinks they are. It was while he was telling me this story that the phone rang. I waved my hand at Meek to make him shut up.

It was Mrs Brigg. She wanted her husband followed again: tomorrow. I said, "But tomorrow's Saturday". She said she knew that and that's what made her suspicious. I asked her what she meant and she told me that her husband was going to a Saturday morning peace meeting, which he had never done before. That, she said, was very fishy which meant I'd have to follow him. I told her I'd do what I could and she said that doing what I could wasn't enough unless it involved following her husband and finding out what he was getting up to and who he was getting up to it with. Now, that was awkward since I'd already promised McJay that I'd go to see the Major in his country abode near Watford. I told Mrs Brigg to hang on a moment and, putting my hand over the telephone mouthpiece, I whispered to

Meek – "You doing anything tomorrow?" He shrugged – "Nothing special." I took my hand off the mouthpiece. "Sorry about that," I said, "I was just checking my appointments. Yes, tomorrow is fine."

"What was all that about?" Meek said when I put the phone down. He was standing by the sink pouring tea into two mugs.

"I've got a job for you."

"Oh yeah?" He sniffed the half-empty bottle of milk and, deciding that it was only slightly sour, poured some of it into the mugs. "And what's brought this about all of a sudden?"

"I've got a job on in Watford tomorrow…"

"Watford?" Meek laughed.

"What's funny about Watford?"

"Nothing funny. Just not my style, if you know what I mean. I went there once. It didn't agree with me. If you want me to do a job in Watford, you can forget it."

From that, I gathered that Meek had made enemies in Watford. Meek was good at making enemies. It was a natural talent of his.

"I don't want you to do a job in Watford," I said. "I'm going to Watford. That's why I can't do the other job."

"What other job would that be?"

"Willow Street."

A lascivious smile broke out on Meek's face. "That's where Kitty Brigg lives."

"It's also where her husband lives. Frankie Brigg. It's Frankie I want you to keep an eye on. In fact, when he leaves the house I want him followed."

Meek glanced over my shoulder. "Tactile," he said.

I was baffled. I had no idea what he was talking about.

"Number 7 Down," he explained. "'Touchy feline reverses into old hat.' Feline is Cat. Reversed is Tac. Touchy is Tactile. Easy."

I looked at my crossword. It all fitted. Then I looked at Meek. "How did you figure that out?"

"I'm not as dim as you think I am."

"So where's the old hat come into it?"

"Tile," he said. "That's what they used to call hats. In the olden days."

"Did they? I'll have to take your word for that." I filled the letters into the empty squares. It drives me nuts when someone figures out a crossword clue that's had me stumped. It especially drives me nuts when that someone is Meek.

"What time will this geezer be leaving the house, then?" Meek asked.

"Does it matter?"

"'Course it matters."

"Ten o'clock in the morning, give or take a few minutes."

"The morning's ok. The afternoon's off, obviously."

"Oh, obviously." I hoped Meek noticed the sneer in my voice. I couldn't think of any reason why tomorrow afternoon would be a problem. Then again, I'm not a sports fan and so I must have been one of the very few people in Britain who hadn't noticed that there was a football match on.

"Yeah," Meek said. "I can follow him. Is that all?"

"Yes, that's all. Why? Is it too menial a task for you now that you've learnt to memorise car numberplates? Incidentally, how many did you get? The numberplates, I mean. The ones you jotted down. When you went to check them, how many numbers did you get right?"

"Impossible to tell."

"Why?"

"All the cars I'd remembered had gone. There were different cars where they'd been. Different cars with different numberplates."

I gritted my teeth. I wasn't sure I was doing the right thing by getting Meek to follow Frankie Brigg. An awful lot could go wrong. But since I wasn't available to do it myself, I didn't have much choice in the matter."

I opened a desk drawer and took a ring-bound pad of paper out of it. "Here!" I threw the pad to Meek. "You'd better take notes."

11. Room 2A

A few minutes after Meek had left, taking with him the ring-bound notepad, I realised that he'd forgotten to take the hideous statuette. The glazed eyes of the little shepherdess and her diabolical lamb glowered at me with malicious intent.

I considered what to do with the rest of the day. I'd finished the crossword, the cat was asleep and the fly was hiding where I couldn't swat it. Operating on sound business principles I should have stayed in the office in the hope that a new client would pop through the door. But, I told myself, clients weren't thick on the ground at the moment. Anyway, I already had two, or maybe three, jobs on the go (I wasn't sure if the job I was doing for McJay counted as a different job from the one I was doing for Major Willoughby-Styrt), which surely meant that my time would be better spent investigating one of them. Besides which, the sun was shining, the birds were singing and I was seized by an irresistible urge to have an afternoon out in leafy Kilburn.

I hopped on the tube, changed at Baker Street and Paddington, and eventually got off at Kilburn Park. From there it was a ten minute walk to the building I'd been watching the night before. I cursed McJay all the way. Up to that moment, I hadn't taken the Major's job seriously. I'd had no intention of putting much effort into trying to find the lowlife scum who'd nicked his top-secret toilet roll inventories. Following Kitty Brigg's erring husband was more in my preferred line of work. But the little detail of the man who'd been killed with a Fairbairn-Sykes knife intrigued me. McJay had known it would. I took the bait, hook, line and sinker.

The Fairbairn-Sykes knife is a nasty bit of kit. It has a seven inch double-edged blade that tapers to a thin, sharp point. It was designed for one purpose and one purpose only: to kill. In the hands of an expert, it does that very efficiently. It can be used for slashing or stabbing, with a frontal or rear attack. Due to its double-edged blade and finely honed point, stabbing is its speciality. The simplest targets are the throat, stomach, kidneys or arteries. Most professionals would go for an artery. A thrust and twist to the jugular is quick but messy due to the sheer amount of blood produced. A stab to the heart or one of its adjacent arteries has the benefit of being just as quick but a lot less messy. It's also hard to do. The only way to do it successfully is to push the blade between the ribs at just the right point. Unless you are very lucky indeed, the chances of finding exactly the right place when launching a quick attack on someone would be extremely poor. To have any chance of bringing it off you'd need to be facing the target, talking to him maybe, sizing him up, working out exactly the place in his ribcage where you could push home the knife and exactly the right angle where it would do the most damage. According to McJay, Corporal Welbridge was killed by a single thrust between the fourth and fifth ribs. Which meant that either his killer was an expert with the knife or else he had been extremely lucky.

The Fairbairn-Sykes knife was first used during the Second World War and it's still occasionally used to this day. If Corporal Welbridge was killed with a Fairbairn-Sykes knife, it was odds-on that it was a soldier or an ex-soldier who had killed him. That didn't narrow the field all that much. In principle, almost any soldier might have been trained to use the knife. In practice, not many would have been. Unless they had been commandos or had been in one of the more secretive "special operations" units. Of those who had been trained in its use, most wouldn't have been able to use it kill a man as quickly and efficiently as the person who'd bumped off Corporal Welbridge. That was the work of an expert.

I couldn't figure out what, if anything, the killing of Corporal Welbridge had to do with the Major's misplaced toilet rolls. All I knew for sure was that McJay wanted me to take the Major's problem more seriously than I had been taking it and he was prepared to pay me to do so. Money for old rope.

On Saturday morning I'd take a train to a village called Little Froomly, not far from Watford, and there I would spend a lovely day with Major Willoughby-Styrt and his fragrant wife. McJay had made the arrangements and the Major was expecting me. Meanwhile, I still had the rest of Friday afternoon to get through.

It was pleasantly warm and the sun shone picturesquely on the ugly old building in the backstreets of Kilburn. The front door was open so I went in and trotted briskly up to the first floor. The door to Room 2B was locked. Next to Room 2B was, not entirely surprisingly, Room 2A. According to the plaque by the door, 2A was the premises of a Christian Evangelical publishing house. The door was slightly ajar so I tapped on it and, when a thin, reedy voice told me to come in, that's what I did.

A small, squirrel-like woman with her grey hair tied in a tight bun emerged from behind some stacks of books towering over her. "Ah!" Her face broke into a broad smile. "West Africa!" she said.

"I beg your pardon?"

"Reverend Pillingham sent you, I presume?"

I assured her that he had not.

"Oh. So you won't be collecting five hundred inspirational tracts for the Sierra Leonean mission?"

"If I did that," I said, "I suspect Reverend Pillingham would not be well pleased."

"Quite so! Quite so!" she chirruped. "And I should not like to be on the wrong side of Reverend Pillingham when he is displeased. Do you know him, by any chance?"

I informed her that I had not had that pleasure.

"West Bromwich, you know. Lovely man. But not to be trifled with. Heavyweight champion. Boxing."

"Ah?"

"Before he took the cloth, of course. Now then, sir, how may I help you?"

"I was looking for the gentleman in the office next door."

"Next door?"

"Room 2B."

"There is a gentleman there, you say?"

"Not at the moment. I was wondering if you would know where he might be."

"Not the foggiest idea, I'm afraid. Never seen him. Not once. And I've been here three years."

"Really? Why?"

"Yes, really. As to why – do you mean why have I been here for three years or why have I never seen the man in the adjoining office?"

"The latter."

"That, I fear, is a question which I cannot answer. The office remains permanently locked. No, that is not quite true. Occasionally, some men arrive with boxes. They take boxes in. And sometimes they take boxes out. I don't think the men with the boxes own the business, however. I don't wish to seem rude, but I have the impression that they lack… now how can I put this?"

"Business acumen?" I suggested.

"Exactly! Well-phrased, sir. It avoids saying that they appear to be congenitally stupid, which they do, but which, to put into words, lacks Christian charity. Yes, yes, 'business acumen' is most certainly what they lack."

"Ah well, I'm sorry to have troubled you," I said, as I headed towards the door.

"Oh, before you go," she chirruped.

"Yes?"

"I was wondering whether you might care to purchase a small booklet on the life of Saint Jerome?"

The smile froze on my face. I was just about to tell her that purchasing a small booklet on the life of Saint Jerome was something that I definitely would not care to do, but there was something about the pleading look in her eyes that penetrated through my crusty outer shell and before I knew what I was doing I was handing over a half-crown coin.

"To be quite frank," she whispered, as she handed the book to me, "I suspect that the owner of the business next door may be, how shall I put it, somewhat shady?"

"Oh yes? In what way?"

"Perhaps I am being cynical but I shouldn't be at all surprised if they turned out to be Seventh Day Adventists!"

12. Room 1B

If anyone could enlighten me about the fashionable young man from Room 2B it was the occupant of Room 1B who, according to the sign next to the door, was one Irena Duvere "(appointments only)". When I'd been watching the building on the previous evening, Rooms 2B and 1B had been the only rooms with lights on. Maybe Irena worked at night. In which case, maybe she knew something about what went on in Room 2B on Thursday evenings.

Then again, if she worked at night, maybe she stayed up late, maybe into the early of hours of the next morning. Some jobs are like that. In which case it was quite possible that on a Friday afternoon she'd be catching up on her sleep and if I knocked at her door and woke her up, she'd be pretty damn' pissed off with me. I knocked anyway.

After a few moments the door opened a crack and through that crack peered two deep green eyes set in a face that looked like it should have been on a movie poster. The voice didn't fit the face. "Can I help you?" it said. It was like hearing Gina Lollobrigida speaking with a Bermondsey accent.

"Irena Duvere?" I said.

She nodded. "And who are you?"

I told her.

"And what do you want from me, Mr Kennick?"

"I'm looking for someone."

"Oh!"

I realised that my words might be open to more than one interpretation, so I added quickly, "A man."

"Ah."

I realised that my words were now open to even more interpretations. I needed to be more specific. "The man upstairs. Room 2B. 'Baron's Fine Living'."

"Oh. Simon Baron. Are you a friend of his?"

Irena opened the door a bit. She cut quite a figure. On the whole I was glad I hadn't put Meek on this job. Meek gets distracted by women like Irena. Whereas I have a business to run so I look over the sights with the icy detachment of a tour guide.

"No," I said. "Not a friend."

"A business associate?"

"Well. Not exactly that either."

There was an awkward pause. I filled the gap by taking a closer look at Irena. Going from the floor up, I saw black stilettoes, a tight black skirt that showed plenty of leg, a tight red blouse that showed plenty of cleavage, big golden earrings, curly black hair, red lipstick and smouldering green eyes. She stood in the doorway, blocking my view of her room. From what little I saw, the interior decoration involved a lot of red silk and velvet drapery. I couldn't see much though because the lighting was so dim.

"Do you ever see Simon Baron?" I asked.

"He and I work similar hours, I think. Evenings, I mean."

"Can I come in?"

"No. I have a client."

"I thought you said you worked evenings."

"I'm flexible."

"You live here?"

"Are you from the council?"

"No."

"The landlord?"

"No."

"These are business premises. I don't live here. I run my business here. Sometimes in the afternoons. Mostly in the evenings. If you're not from the council and you're not from the landlord, what's it matter to you?"

"I wondered if you might know Simon Baron. That's all."

She smouldered at me a bit, the way she might smoulder at a spider just before treading on it. Then she decided I might not be the most verminous specimen she'd ever seen – not as bad as someone from the council or the landlord, at any rate – and she relaxed.

"Simon Baron. I wonder why you are so interested in Simon Baron? You don't look like the chaps he usually has dealings with."

"What sort of chaps does he usually have dealings with?"

"Villains."

"What's his business exactly?"

She laughed. It was a throaty laugh with a hint of cigarette smoke. "You tell me! A bit of this, a bit of that, if you know what I mean."

"His company's called 'Baron's Fine Living'. What's that? Furniture? Food?"

"Anything that makes a good living for Simon Baron, I reckon. Knickknacks mostly."

"Knickknacks?"

"That's what he told me, the only time I ever bothered asking him. A few weeks ago it was. Some chaps were lugging cardboard boxes up to his office. They seemed to be heavy. I happened to be going out at the time and I bumped into Simon in the foyer. I said 'What you got in them boxes? Gold bars?' He laughed and said, 'I wish! Just knickknacks, that's all is in them boxes. Ornaments. Curios. Trinkets.'"

I was reminded of the shepherd statue that Meek had bought in the Petticoat Lane. Not much money in those, I thought. Not unless there was an endless supply of customers as undiscerning as Meek.

"He doesn't strike me as the sort of fellow who'd deal in trinkets," I said.

"That's what I think too." Clearly we had both formed the opinion that Simon Baron was not quite on the level; that he was, in fact, decidedly on the dodgy side.

"He never works days?" I asked.

"I've only ever seen him in the evenings. Him and some other people. Weekends mostly. Thursday, Friday, sometimes Saturday."

"And Monday?"

"No. Never on a Monday. Not that I've noticed anyhow. Not that I'm always here on Mondays myself. Not my busiest evening, Monday."

"Were you here last Monday evening?"

"As a matter of fact I was. And the Monday before that. That's the way my business goes. You never can tell. Anyway, Simon wasn't here. His room is right above mine. I hear their footsteps. And sometimes scraping sounds."

"What kind of scraping sounds?"

"Boxes. Tea-chests. That sort of thing."

"Full of knickknacks?"

She smiled broadly. "So I suppose."

"Has Simon Baron ever…" I hesitated. I glanced into her room. She got my meaning.

"Has Simon been a client of mine?" She laughed. "No. He's not the sort."

"Oh?"

She opened the door wider so I could see the room more clearly. There was a big table at the centre, covered in a dark velvet cloth. Crouched next to the table in a velvet-covered chair was a plump woman wearing a shapeless brown hat fixed to her head with hatpins. Irena pulled the door shut again.

"Your client?" I said.

She gave that throaty, smoky chuckle of hers again. "You seem surprised. What did you think my business was? I'm a clairvoyant, Mr Kennick. I tell people what lies in their future."

"Oh yes?" I smiled. "So what lies in mine?"

She smiled back. "If you want to know that, you'll have to make an appointment."

13. SABOTAGE

"Damn' nuisance the lot of them!"

We were standing in a field, a few miles outside the village of Little Froomly to the north of Watford. There was a short box-like, concrete construction, almost waist-high, sticking out of the grass. On the top of the concrete box there was a metal hatch which should have been securely locked but was not. Major Edward Willoughby-Styrt was holding the padlock in his hands. The chain to which the padlock had been attached was lying loose on the ground. One of its links had just been cut by a tall young man named Ronnie Dickens who was standing alongside, holding a pair of long-handled bolt-cutters. He was sweating from his recent exertion.

"Of course, we've tried to stop them," the Major continued. "But how can we? This place is irregularly manned. A couple of the chaps come here once or twice a week to make sure everything is in working order. But it's only fully manned when we have a training exercise, which we have but seldom. So, you see, those damn' vandals have plenty of opportunity to sneak up and cause whatever irresponsible damage they choose to. I've reported them to the police, of course, but they say there's nothing they can do about it. Can you believe that? Nothing they can do about it! If I had my way, something would be done about it once and for all. Those long-haired layabouts are no better than foxes that steal a farmer's eggs. And we know damn' well what the farmer does about that!"

The Major chuckled at his own joke. Maybe I'd misjudged him when I'd said he had no sense of humour. The idea of shooting a lot of "long-haired layabouts" (as he fondly called them) brought tears of mirth to his eyes. He objected to long-haired layabouts in general. But he particularly objected to the local long-haired layabouts who were affiliated with some sort of nuclear disarmament group. For their part, it appeared that the local long-haired layabouts harboured equally strong objections to the Major and, indeed, to anyone who was involved with the Royal Observer Corps whose bunker we were at that moment standing alongside.

The bunker was nothing more than a small underground room which could be accessed by opening the hatch and climbing down a vertical ladder. When the bunker was not in use, the hatch was locked using the padlock that the Major was currently holding. Someone had poured glue into the lock, so that the key would not fit into it. Which is why Ronnie Dickens, a local garage mechanic, had gone to get his bolt-cutters in order to cut through the chain that secured the lock.

"Why did they do it?" I asked. I was genuinely curious to know the answer. From what little I knew of the Royal Observer Corps – the ROC – they were largely a volunteer organisation; just ordinary, well-meaning people trying to prepare for the worst.

"To hear those pacifist chaps talk, you'd think that we were the enemy, rather than the Soviets," the Major said. "If the bomb drops it won't be an RAF plane that drops it. But that's not the way they see it. They have this bizarre idea that any contingency planning on our part is somehow responsible for increasing the likelihood of nuclear conflict. So they do everything in their power to frustrate us. Pouring glue into the lock is the least of it. They shout at us, they put up highly offensive posters in town. On one occasion they painted swastikas on my wife's gnomes."

"Her gnomes?"

"In the garden. She has three of them. One has a fishing rod, one pushes a wheelbarrow and one sits on a toadstool smoking a pipe. They even painted a toothbrush moustache on the gnome sitting on the toadstool! Bloody anarchists, that's what they are!"

It occurred to me that the Major seemed to be more worried about peace protestors with posters and glue than he was about the Soviets with their H-Bombs.

"Still," I said, "if glue is the worst we have to worry about, that's an improvement over the last time."

He looked at me uncomprehendingly, so I reminded him about the unfortunate death of Corporal Welbridge at the exercise in Hackney.

"Yes, well..." He gave the impression that this was a subject about which he did not wish to speak. "Most unfortunate, most unfortunate. But these things happen, you know."

I wasn't sure whether he didn't know that Welbridge had been murdered or whether he assumed that I didn't know.

"You knew him well?"

"Who?"

"Welbridge. Corporal Welbridge."

"No. Not at all. Well, by sight, I suppose. Yes, yes, most tragic. Most tragic."

I would have liked to ask him more on the subject but I got the feeling that it would have been a waste of time. If he knew anything about Corporal Welbridge or the circumstances of his death, he did not think I was a suitable person with whom to discuss such matters.

"Shall I blow the whistle now, sir? Oh, it's you again, Mr Kennick! I didn't expect to see you here." At first I didn't recognise the young woman addressing me. She was wearing a green silk blouse and a pair of tan slacks tucked into black Wellington boots; her sandy-coloured hair was tied in a ponytail. It was her rather musical voice that gave her away. This was the same woman who had been wearing a nurse's uniform in the exercise at Hackney.

"I didn't expect to see you here either," I said. "So which are you, really? A nurse or a fashion model?"

She frowned. "That's a very condescending attitude, you know. Somewhat old-fashioned, if you don't mind my saying. This is the modern world, Mr Kennick."

"I'm sorry. In the good old days – five or six years ago, say – women rather liked to be complimented."

"We still do. For something that's worthy of your compliment. I don't think the 'fashion model' line is quite the thing, though. It makes you sound somewhat debauched."

"Ah." Duly chastised, I adopted a more serious tone. "You weren't just acting the part, then? The nurse, I mean. Like all those people acting the parts of the dead and dying?"

"Good heavens, no! I work at the local cottage hospital. I'm not on duty today, however. And it might surprise you to know that we nurses tend not to wear the uniform in our spare time. The more pertinent question, I should have thought, is why are *you* here. You're not local, that's for sure. Did I hear someone say you were from the Ministry?"

The Major interrupted before I had a chance to reply. "Mr Kennick is helping us with some administrative matters, Miss Barrington."

"Ah. I see. Administrative matters. That covers rather a lot, I should imagine." She held out her hand. "I don't think we've been properly introduced, Mr Kennick. Briony Barrington."

I shook her hand. "So how did you become involved in all this, Miss Barrington?"

"There, you see. You are being old-fashioned again. Nobody calls me Miss Barrington."

"The Major…" I turned to where he had been standing but he was no longer there. He was striding over towards a small group of men of whose military discipline he was being loudly critical.

"The Major called you Miss Barrington," I said.

"Ha! But he's terribly old and venerable, isn't he. You're not so far gone as that, I shouldn't think. At any rate, call me Briony. In answer to your question, my involvement here is all down to that young man." She nodded towards Ronnie Dickens, who was still holding the bolt-cutters. "We're quite chummy, as you might say. Ronnie's an ROC observer. So I sort of took up his hobby."

An odd hobby, I thought. Practising for Armageddon. Rehearsing for the end of the world.

Suddenly, Briony Barrington put a whistle to her lips and blew a penetrating note that made my ears ring. "Sorry about that," she said. "It's a bit loud, isn't it. It's just that some of the chaps down there were straying." She was referring to a small group of people wandering around at the far end of the sloping field. "Teddy, the Major I mean, is going to give them a bit of a briefing, you see. What to do if the macaroons go off and all that."

"Macaroons?" I said.

"That's what I call them. You know, like the coconut cakes. They're really called maroons. They're like big Roman Candles. You fire them into the air and they go off with an almighty bang to warn us that a nuclear bomb has been dropped and we should all hide under the kitchen table."

"Wouldn't the nuclear bomb make a pretty big bang all on its own?"

"You would have thought so, wouldn't you? I think the maroons are supposed to warn people who are far enough away from the bomb not to have noticed it. Then we are supposed to protect ourself from the fallout – radioactive dust and whatnot. Mind you, that's all a bit theoretical as far as Little Froomly is concerned since we haven't any maroons."

It was then that I saw another familiar face. Warden Featherglade, the officious little man who had complained that my name wasn't on his damn' list on the day of the exercise in Bully Fen. He was gasping and wheezing as he strode up the hill towards us. Well, I say "hill" but it was really no more than a gentle rise across a grassy field. From the way he was puffing and panting, you'd think it was the north face of the Eiger. He was still wearing his warden's uniform but on this occasion he had omitted the metal helmet with the "W" on the front. I took this as a sign that he didn't think any bombs were likely to be dropped imminently.

"Luckily, we do have Warden Featherglade," Briony said. "I am told that when the bomb drops, since we have no maroons, he will run up and down the High Street blowing a whistle."

"The Soviets don't know what they are up against," I said, encouragingly.

Briony laughed, "It's the running aspect of it that bothers me. I very much doubt if Warden Featherglade has run anywhere in his entire life. Running the whole length of the High Street may be more than he could take."

By this time, Warden Featherglade had completed his ascent of the field and was fast approaching the ROC post where we were assembled. The Major, having detached himself from the small group of men whom he'd been lecturing on discipline, escorted Featherglade over the final few yards. I called out a cheery "Hello" and Featherglade replied with a grunt which was the nearest to "Hello" that he could manage in his state of extreme exhaustion.

"Featherglade is in charge of the observation post," the Major explained. "He's a good man. Reliable, you know. Our chief observer here. Which is why I asked him up today. It's best if he shows you around."

I should probably explain why I was being given the guided tour. It wasn't because I was interested in seeing at first-hand how the villagers of Little Froomly might help to save Britain in the event of nuclear annihilation. It was because I was trying to retrace the Major's steps on Sunday the 17th of July which was the only time, as far as I could gather, when the documents which had been stolen might have been both out of his house and out of his sight. The Major had given me a brief outline of the events of the day in question as we had walked over the fields towards the ROC bunker. In fact, I already knew most of those details, since I had previously been briefed by McJay. Piecing together McJay's account with the Major's, this is what I knew about the goings on in and around Little Froomly on the dates between Friday the 15th of July, when the documents were placed into the Major's attaché case, and Monday the 18th of July when they were discovered to be there no longer:

On Friday the 15th of July, after leaving his office in Whitehall, Major Edward Willoughby-Styrt travelled from London to his home in Little Froomly. He made the journey in his car, a cream-coloured Daimler V8, and took with him an attaché case containing some documents which he planned to study over the weekend. That weekend, however, two notable events took place in the vicinity of the village. On the Saturday, the annual village fête was held in the grounds of the vicarage; it involved tombolas, cake-baking and vegetable-growing competitions and a performance by the local folk group. The Major's wife attended the fête but the Major stayed at home to do work of such national importance that he felt unable to confide its details to me. Thus, neither the Major nor the attaché case left the house that day.

The following day, Sunday the 17th of July, in the afternoon, there was a training exercise at the ROC observation post, in a scrubby field, about a mile outside the village itself. Coincidentally, the gardening society had its annual flower show in the village hall that same afternoon and this was attended by the Major's wife. While his wife was in the village hall, the Major came to the ROC exercise, bringing with him his attaché case, since he felt that the documents would be safer if they were kept with him at all times rather than being left in the empty house. The exercise involved a simulated nuclear attack in the vicinity of Watford (why the Soviets regarded Watford as a prime military target was a mystery that was not explained to me) and required some people in the observation post to observe and then report the attack to higher authorities after which various wardens went about doing whatever wardens did in such circumstances to ensure the safety of the local inhabitants.

At six o'clock, the Major returned home. He and his wife spent the evening watching television (there was a particularly gripping episode of Perry Mason, the Major informed me). They went to bed at half past nine and, the following morning, the Major and his attaché case returned to his office in Whitehall.

It was only on the Monday morning that the absence of certain documents was noticed. One of the Major's superiors requested to see a particular document. The Major's assistant, Gregory O'Donnell, asked the Major for that document. The Major took a folder from his attaché case and passed it across to O'Donnell. It was then that O'Donnell discovered that several of the documents were missing.

From the time when the Major had left his office on the Friday afternoon to time when he had returned on the Monday morning, his attaché case had been with him at all times. Of course, if that were literally true, the only person who could have removed the missing documents was the Major himself. I put this to him bluntly. He raised his eyebrows at me and told me that I should be very careful indeed about making accusations for which I had no proof. I smiled sweetly and explained that it was not an accusation, it was a logical deduction. He thought about this for a few moments, accepted that my reasoning was sound, and added, "Actually, there may have been an odd moment. When. You know."

I smiled enigmatically and said nothing.

He cleared his throat and continued: "What I mean to say is that, there may have been a fleeting moment when… well, when the attaché case may have been…well, you know how it is."

"No, I don't know how it is," I replied. "Not until you tell me."

"Out of my sight," he said. "What I'm trying to say is that it is possible that the attaché case may have been out of my sight for a brief interlude."

"Possible?" I said. "You mean, you can't be sure."

"Well, now I think of it, yes, yes, I am quite certain. I recall that I was down in the bunker checking the logbook entries. They keep a logbook to verify any observations they may have to make, you understand."

"Observations? Of nuclear bombs, you mean."

"Precisely."

I didn't pursue that line of enquiry. Had any nuclear bombs been dropped near Watford, I assumed I would already have heard about them.

"Then one of the chaps called down the hatch. Ronnie Dickens, I think it was. Said there was a pornographic photograph in the GZI and wanted to know what he should do about it."

"The GZI?"

"The Ground Zero Indicator. It's a gizmo we have above ground. A sort of metal cylinder with small holes punched into the sides, like a pinhole camera. When a nuclear bomb goes off, it takes a photograph."

"You think the GZI took a pornographic photograph?" I said. The Major gave me a disapproving look to indicate that my levity was distasteful to him.

"Every ROC post has a GZI, you see. When the time comes we will be able to telephone our coordinates through to HQ. They will triangulate them and that will tell them the exact location of the bomb blast."

I couldn't help thinking that when an H-Bomb goes off, there are more obvious ways of telling its location than by triangulating pinhole photographs. But I didn't think that observation would be well received so I smiled grimly and tried to look impressed.

"At any rate, when Dickens told me about the business with the GZI, I scrambled up the ladder to take a look. There was no photographic paper in the device. Someone had replaced it with a sordid picture cut from a magazine which, I am told, goes by the name of 'Parade'. It was sabotage, of course. The same people who glued up the padlock today, I have no doubt. So I told Dickens not to worry, that I'd have more supplies sent along a-s-a-p. Then I scrambled back down into the bunker to complete my inspection of the log. The attaché case was next to the logbook but it can't have been out of my sight for more than a minute. And, really, how could anyone have slipped down there in that time without my seeing them?"

The Major had told me all this just before Warden Featherglade and Briony Barrington had arrived. I didn't want to continue our conversation in front of them. So I suggested that it might be useful if I were given a guided tour of the bunker.

"I'll show you around, Mr Kennick," said Warden Featherglade, officiously.

"Good man!" said the Major. "You are in capable hands, Mr Kennick. Featherglade knows far more about the workings of the monitoring post than I do."

If I had any reservations about being left in Featherglade's capable hands, the Major didn't give me any opportunity to express them. No sooner had he finished speaking than he and Briony Barrington turned on their heels and were already striding away across the field in the direction of the village, leaving just the three of us – Featherglade, Ronnie Dickens and me – standing next to the opening to the bunker.

14. Into The Bunker

"Well now, sir, shall we descend?" Warden Featherglade was showing his friendly side to me that morning. On the whole, I preferred his grumpy side.

"After you," I replied.

"There's quite a bit to it, of course. The technicalities will be above the head of a layman, so to speak." He gave me a comforting smile. "I'll simplify it for you."

He opened the metal hatch and down he went with me following, clambering awkwardly down the metal ladder that was fixed to a wall of the entrance shaft. The shaft was quite narrow and Featherglade just about filled it. I felt like a Victorian chimney sweep. All that was missing was the soot. The distance from the raised access hatch to the underground floor of the bunker must have been about nine or ten feet. Once I had arrived in the subterranean room, there really wasn't all that much to see.

It was a small, bare room with whitewashed walls. There was a table and a couple of bunk beds against the far wall. On the wall there was a clock and a radio and some kind of electronic device that looked a bit like a tape-recorder and another thing that looked like a big speedometer. Featherglade explained what they all were but I didn't pay much attention. Apparently the basic idea was that when a bomb went off in the vicinity, one of the people in the bunker would clamber up the ladder, go outside and take a reading from the Ground Zero Indicator. Then he'd come back down again, quite possibly trailing clouds of radioactive dust, and (assuming the phone lines were still working) he would phone through to HQ.

When, after what seemed like hours, Featherglade finally paused to take a breath, I mentioned the ROC training exercise of July the 17th. I wanted to check the Major's version of events. "Major Willoughby-Styrt came down into this bunker, to check the logbook, I gather?"

Featherglade pursed his lips and frowned as though he was trying to solve a difficult crossword clue. Then he ventured an exploratory smile. "Ha!" he said. "Logbook!" he added.

"Yes, the logbook," I said. "Can I take a look at it?"

"The logbook! Ha!" His little smile broadened as though he had just understood the punchline to a particularly convoluted joke. "Now why would we keep a logbook?"

"To log details of the bombs?" I suggested.

"Bombs! Ha! Yes. That's a good one. Bombs. Ha, ha! Bombs in Little Froomly. That's a good one that is."

If he had understood the joke, I hadn't. "That's the whole point of the bunker, isn't it?"

"When hostilities break out, as it were, the bunker will be fully manned. Oh yes. Night and day. Three men down here until the fallout has passed and we are instructed to go above ground, as it were. But, at present, of course, the bunker is not manned. It is purely kept in readiness. When the time comes, we shall keep a most detailed logbook. Until that unhappy day, however…"

"No logbook?"

"No logbook."

"So why did the Major come down here?"

"Tea."

"I beg your pardon."

"I made some tea. The Major joined me. We had a mug of tea each. And also some Garibaldi biscuits."

"Ah," I said. I didn't think this conversation was getting me anywhere. On the spur of the moment, an idea came into my head. It was a longshot but worth trying. "What is Turnstile?" I asked.

Featherglade recoiled as though he'd received a small electric shock. He recovered his composure quickly, however, and said, "The name means nothing to me."

That was an odd thing to say, I thought. If it had meant nothing to him, I'd have expected him to say "I don't know," or "Never heard of it," or something similar. After all, Turnstile sounds more like a thing than a person, an anonymous object rather than something with a name. And yet Featherglade told me "the name" meant nothing to him. Which made me think that it meant quite a lot to him but whatever it was he didn't want to tell me. I shrugged it off. "I overheard someone mention it," I said as though it was no more than a matter of idle curiosity to me.

15. Gnomes and Cucumber Sandwiches

Not for the first time, I wondered why I had even bothered to take on this job. The answer, of course, was money. It might be a wild goose chase but I was getting paid to do it.

"Featherglade told me that the bunker is intended to be manned by three people," I said. The Major was driving me back to the village in his car – a smart, if rather showy, cream-coloured Daimler. I let myself sink into the embrace of the dove-grey, leather upholstered seat. "Was anyone alone in the bunker with your attaché case?"

"I don't recall. There were people around, of course. Only Featherglade was down there when I went to check the logbook, I think."

That non-existent logbook again!

"Why?" he asked. "Surely you don't think that Featherglade… No, that's absurd. The man is as honest as the day is long."

"But could someone else have gone down there?"

"Oh, perhaps. There were a few chaps going through the protocols, all that sort of thing."

"What protocols might those be?"

"Oh. The things to be done, you know. In the event of an attack. Do you really need to know all that?"

"And in the event of an attack there would be three people in the bunker. Those would be who? Featherglade and two others, I suppose?"

"Impossible to know. It would all depend on who was available at the time of the attack. You see, while the bunker is intended for three people, they are not invariably the same three."

"They aren't?"

"Certainly not. We have a team of twelve volunteers. We divide them into four teams."

"Why twelve?"

He raised his eyebrows at me. It was a gesture that irritated me more every time he did it. "We cannot know who will be available when the bomb drops, Mr Kennick. Some may be at work, or on holiday. Some may be ill. Some may, of course, already be dead. It would be much more convenient for us if the Soviets did the decent thing by giving us advance warning. But I think that's rather unlikely, don't you?"

"Oh, rather!" I agreed and I raised my eyebrows at him. My eyebrow-raising technique was clearly not of the same calibre as the Major's. The expression on his face suggested that he thought I might be a congenital idiot.

"So," I went on, "on the day of the exercise, which three men were manning the bunker?"

"Featherglade, of course. Also Ronnie Dickens whom you've met. And a chap named Thomas Ritting whom you have not met due to the fact that he is currently on holiday in Eastbourne. But I have complete trust in all three men. I hope you are not suggesting that one of them might have purloined the documents. No, no, that really won't do. Quite out of the question. They are men of unassailable probity, I assure you."

"Was the attaché case locked?" I asked.

"Certainly it was. When we get back to my cottage you shall see it for yourself."

On the short journey from the field containing the ROC post to the Major's country dwelling, he pointed out the notable landmarks, such as there were. At the entrance to the village stood a miserable-looking grey-stone building which I was informed was the vicarage. It was in the vicarage gardens that the village fair had been held on the day prior to the ROC exercise. Just beyond the vicarage was a pub called The Jolly Ploughman, then there was a school, some poky little shops and a dreary little village green. The village hall, where the Major's wife had attended the flower show on the afternoon of the ROC exercise, overlooked the green. In other words, Little Froomly was a very ordinary little village, not much different from hundreds of other ordinary little villages spread out across the length and breadth of England.

The Major's "cottage", which was called The Coombes, was at the other end of the village. As this was such an ordinary little English village, I was expecting the Major's home to be an ordinary little English cottage – the sort, with whitewashed walls, rambling roses and a picturesque thatched roof. In fact, it was a huge, blocky 19th Century construction that looked as though it might once have been a correctional facility for unruly boys or an asylum for the criminally insane. Its austere façade had been softened by the addition of some wisteria clambering up a trellis. The garden around the house must have taken up a couple of acres; it featured formal flower beds and a few gnarly apple trees.

The inside of the house had the sort of muffled silence that only expensive Axminster carpets can provide. The sole intrusion into the silence was the soft ticking of the grandfather clock in the hallway. The Major led me into an elegant, oak-panelled room that smelled of freshly-picked flowers and beeswax. A smart woman with an upright bearing was standing there, waiting for us. She wore a long, floral dress and a refined smile.

Introductions were made ("My wife," said the Major. "But please call me Marjory," added his wife) and then a young woman wearing a long grey dress entered and asked if we would be taking tea. "We shall take it here, Helen," Marjory told her. Once Helen had left the room, Marjory, the Major and I sat down in huge armchairs arranged around an elaborately carved coffee table and chatted about the weather for a couple of minutes. Then Helen came back with a tray loaded with a bone china teapot and cups and plates bearing mounds of thin sandwiches cut into triangles. The whole procedure was so correct and precise that it felt as though it had been rehearsed in advance.

While I was drinking tea and nibbling at a cucumber sandwich, Major Willoughby-Styrt suddenly exclaimed, "The attaché case! You wanted to see it, yes?"

I told him I did. He leapt from his chair and left the room. During his absence I made small talk with his wife.

"Have you lived here long?"

"A few years. Would you care for another sandwich?"

"Thank you. They are delicious. Your husband was telling me about your gnomes."

"Gnomes?" She looked perplexed.

"Your garden gnomes. The ones that were defaced."

"Gnomes?" she said again. "You must have misheard, Mr Kennick. I can assure you we have no garden gnomes."

"Ah. I obviously got the wrong end of the stick."

The conversation languished. I nibbled the sandwich. "Lovely house you have," I said. "Beautiful garden."

"Yes. It is."

"Hard to look after all this all on your own, I imagine."

"I have a gardener. Helen helps out with food and suchlike. And I have a girl from the village who does the washing and cleaning."

"You go up to London sometimes, I suppose?"

She smiled. "Never. I hate the place. And my husband has a poky little flat in town whereas here we have this lovely house."

"It must seem very empty, though, with your husband being away all week…"

"He comes home on the weekends."

"On Friday evening? What time does he arrive, if you don't mind my asking?"

"I really don't care what you ask, Mr Kennick. He arrives at about nine o'clock. And on Monday he departs at…"

"He arrived at nine o'clock on Friday the fifteenth?"

"Thereabouts. It's his regular time. I make a light supper and we eat it together. With a glass or two of wine."

"It must be one of the few occasions when the two of you have the opportunity to…"

"Are you concerned that I may be lonely, Mr Kennick? Quite the reverse. We have a range of activities in the village – the local history society, the Women's Institute. We even have a yoga class."

"And the Royal Observer Corps, of course."

"Oh, war games! I leave those to the men."

"Here it is!" The Major re-entered the room, holding in his hands a dark brown, leather attaché case. "Open it!" he said, handing it to me.

It was one of those cases with a little clip-down clasp with a small keyhole above it. The clasp was locked. "How shall I open it?" I said.

"Without the keys you'll find that it is not possible."

At first I thought he was joking. Then I remembered that he was almost totally devoid of a sense of humour. I could have opened that lock with a paperclip. I didn't have a paperclip on me so I handed the case back. "Are there top-secret documents in it at the moment?" I asked.

"If there were," he said, "they would not concern you. All that you need be concerned with is the fact that the case could not have been opened without the key. Not without breaking the lock, that is. And, as you can see, it is not broken. So that suggests to me that the documents must have been abstracted either before I locked the case when leaving my office on the Friday or after I opened the case upon my return on the Monday."

"Did you read the documents over the weekend?"

"As a matter of fact, I did not. The ROC exercises were the focus of my attention."

"So you can't be sure they were ever in the case?"

"That is correct. The folder which should, in principle, have contained the documents, most certainly was in the case. I put it there myself on the Friday afternoon, after my assistant gave it to me. But I did not check its contents."

After I'd finished my tea, Major Willoughby-Styrt insisted on showing me his study, which was a big room containing a vast mahogany desk and a leather chesterfield settee. He told me that his briefcase had been in the study from the evening of Friday the 15th of July until the early morning of Monday the 18th of July when he drove back to London, apart from during the few hours of the ROC exercise.

I walked around his study, gave a cursory glance at the windows and checked their locks as though I thought they might be important. Which I didn't. I asked him if anyone else had been in the house over the weekend – the girl from the village who did the washing and cleaning maybe?

"Why should she have been here? No. Of course not."

"Helen?"

"No."

"Who is Helen, by the way? If you don't mind my asking."

"I don't mind at all, old man, though I don't think it is pertinent to your enquiry. Helen is my wife's companion. She helps with business matters, purchases, expenditures, the general running of the house. She's from a very good family. Quite above suspicion, I assure you."

On the way back to the station, we passed once more through the village green. It was a classic of its type: a square of grass at the centre of which was a small pond with two ducks quacking lazily as they paddled past the plate-like leaves of some waterlilies. The main street of the village forked around the green. On either side of the street stood quaint, old buildings including the white-painted, half-timbered The Jolly Ploughman pub. It was a scene that had, in all probability, changed little in the last century or two. Apart, that is, from the group of people sitting on the grass next to the margin of the pond. There were two men and three women. As far as I could tell, they were all in their early twenties except for one of the men who I'd have said was probably about my age, which is what I like to call "mid-thirties or thereabouts". Both men and two of the girls had shoulder-length hair. The third girl had a boyish Mary Quant-style haircut.

They were all wearing colourful clothes and were either lying full-length or else sitting cross-legged. They were passing around a bottle of Liebfraumilch, a German wine which, in my opinion, tastes only slightly better than petroleum but which the people on the grass showed some indications of enjoying. Maybe their senses had been dulled by what they were smoking which was clearly not tobacco.

"You see what I mean," the Major said, leaning towards me in order to whisper. "Anarchists!"

"These are the peace people?" I asked.

"If I had my way," the Major said, "I'd have them all rounded up and…" He paused.

"Shot?" I suggested.

"Put into the Army," he corrected. "It was, in my opinion, a great mistake to end Conscription so soon. Those young people have never known discipline, so they think nothing of flouting the rules of common decency."

The older man in the group caught sight of the Major and made an unfriendly gesture towards him. The Major snorted. "I am not ignorant of the fact that, to some people, we are figures of fun," he said. "They think we are playing games. But I can assure you, Mr Kennick, that this is no game. If and when the day should come when that fight must indeed be fought, it will be chaps such as Featherglade and women such as Miss Barrington who offer our best last hope."

"Will it work?" I said. I imagined Featherglade running up and down the street blowing his whistle, parents and children hiding under tables, nurses like Briony Barrington dabbing iodine on wounds and putting broken arms in splints.

"What would you do, Mr Kennick?" The Major looked at me. I had no answer to give him. "Would you do nothing?" he said. "Would you, really?"

We were just arriving at the station when suddenly a crowd of people came running down the street towards us shouting at the tops of their voices and waving flags and scarves. It didn't click for a second. Then, out of the roar of their voices, a few recognisable words emerged: "We won!", "Four-two!", "England, England!"

"The World Cup," the Major commented wryly. Since I did not immediately reply, he clarified the remark – "A football match. The final match, I am given to understand, has just taken place."

"I'm guessing the England team won," I said.

The Major shrugged. "I'm a cricket man, myself."

The Major parked his car and moments later we were standing on the platform, waiting for the train to arrive. We had exhausted our principal topics of conversation – namely, the weather (good), the Government (bad), the younger generation (out of control) – and so I filled in a pause with the off-hand remark: "What became of the gnomes?"

"Gnomes?" he said.

"You told me earlier that somebody had defaced your wife's garden gnomes."

"Did I? Did I indeed?"

"You did."

"Ah."

"Your wife told me she didn't have any garden gnomes."

"Ah."

"She didn't seem at all interested in garden gnomes, as far as I could tell."

"No. No. Probably not."

In the distance I could see a train the rumbling along the track towards the station.

"The gnomes," said the Major, "were my little joke."

He didn't laugh. Neither did I.

16. The Disappearing Carrier Bag

It was Monday morning. I had just fed Straker and made a pot of tea when Meek arrived. It was half-past ten. The crack of dawn, as far as Meek was concerned. I assumed he was after money.

"You're after money?" I said.

"What're you on about?"

"In this early. That's the only explanation I can think of."

He picked the cat up off the chair and put him onto the floor. "I'll have some tea if you're making it," he said. "And a custard cream if you've got any."

"You can have tea," I said. "Custard creams cost extra. So if it's not money you're after what is it?"

"I should have thought it's bleedin' obvious."

"I wouldn't be asking if it was obvious."

"The job."

I gave the tea a stir and waited for him to elaborate.

"The job you put me on."

"Oh, that."

Until he'd mentioned it, I'd forgotten all about it. As my Saturday had been taken up with my visit to Little Froomly, I'd given Meek the job of following Frankie Brigg to see if he was really going to a peace meeting or was, on the contrary, engaging in extra-marital shenanigans, as his wife suspected.

"So," I said, handing over a steaming mug of PG Tips, "did you find out anything useful?"

"Useful!" said Meek, then he groaned a bit as Straker leapt onto his lap and dug his claws in. "Useful! More than bleedin' useful, I should say."

Here it comes, I thought. Meek is going to try to touch me for some extra cash. Whatever he's found out, it would be in my financial interests not to seem too thrilled about it. "Oh, yes?" I said. "What?"

"Well, I decided to go there a bit early, didn't I."

"Did you?"

"I did. Half-past nine or thereabouts. In the morning. Which is just as well. Because no sooner had I arrived at his house than out he comes." Meek had the ring-bound notepad that I'd given him open on the desk. He'd filled page after page with notes scrawled with a leaky ballpoint pen. He flipped over a couple of pages and read out what he'd written: "Subject leaves house. Eighteen minutes to ten. Goes to High Street, buys newspaper. The Daily Mirror. And a packet of mint humbugs. Proceeds to bus stop. Waits. Woman approaches. Middle-aged. Grey hair. Says 'Good morning'. Woman with grey hair moves off. Man with dodgy wig arrives, stands behind Subject and asks if he's got the time. Subject looks at his watch and says…"

"Is this relevant?" I asked.

Meek looked insulted. "You told me to make notes."

I didn't remember telling him that. I might have done. Like I'd told him to memorise car numberplates. If he was going to do some investigating, I wanted him to be thorough. I hadn't intended him to write 'War and Peace'.

"Has all that stuff got anything to do with whatever it is you found out about Frankie Brigg that is so important that you came into the office at half-past ten in the morning just to tell me?"

"Who's to say?"

"Just tell me where he went and what he did once he got there."

Meek flipped over a page of his notes. Then he flipped to the page after that.

"Don't bother with your notes for the time being. Just tell me whatever you remember."

"OK. If you're sure."

"I'm sure."

"He went to Croxley."

"Where's Croxley?"

"It's west of Bushey, east of Rickmansworth."

I gave him a blank stare.

"It's on the Metropolitan Line. Not far from Watford, as a matter of fact. You were in Watford on Saturday, weren't you?"

"I passed through it briefly."

Meek shuddered. Whatever experiences he'd had in Watford had clearly scarred him.

"Put me out of my misery," I said. "Why did Frankie Brigg go to Croxley?"

"It's where he works."

"He works on Saturdays?"

"No. His office is shut on Saturday."

"So why did he go there if it's shut?"

"To get something. He went in empty-handed. When he came out, he was holding something."

"What was he holding?"

"I couldn't see. It was in a bag."

"Wait a minute. You said his office was shut on Saturdays. How did he even get inside if the place was locked up? And what about the bag? Where did that come from?"

Meek gave me a look of withering contempt. "If you'd let me read my notes, everything would be clear. I never said it was locked. I said it was shut. Look." He riffled back through his notes and began reading again. "10:33. Subject alights from bus. Walks to M and W C."

"What?"

"M and W C. It's an abbreviation. It took too long to write the whole thing in the notebook. So I shortened it."

"Well, lengthen it again."

"Martin and Whipston Chemicals."

"Which is…?"

"Where he works."

"I thought he was an accountant."

"I don't know what he is. All I know is he went into this place with a sign on the gate that said 'Martin and Whipston Chemicals'."

"And what exactly is Martin and Whipston Chemicals?"

"At a guess I'd say it might be a Chemicals company. Maybe it's run by some geezers called Martin and Whipston? Anyway, that was at 10:43."

"I thought you said it was 10:33."

"He alighted from the bus at 10:33. It's a ten minute walk to this chemicals place. I can give you more details if you like. At 10:34, Subject crosses road and nearly bumps into woman with poodle. At

10:35, Subject goes into sweetshop and buys packet of chewing gum. At 10:37…"

"Get back to the chemical place. He arrives there."

"At 10:43."

"Then what does he do?"

What it boiled down to was this: on Saturday morning Frankie Brigg left home and took a bus to the Martin and Whipston Chemicals company, which is housed in a bleak, box-like building surrounded by a chain-link fence in a place called Croxley. Brigg had a word with a uniformed security man at the gate who waved him through. Ten minutes later, Brigg came out again holding a carrier bag. Then he got onto another bus, which took him to the Hatch End tube station. From there he took a train to Kilburn.

"Kilburn!" I said. At last we were getting somewhere. "Let me guess where he went." I gave Meek a description of the old three-storey building from which I'd seen Frankie Brigg leave in the company of a blonde girl on the previous Thursday evening. The building in which, among other things, is found the offices of a certain Simon Baron. Meek confirmed that the building to which Frankie Brigg had gone on Saturday fitted that description.

"I watched him go in," he said. "And ten minutes later, he came out. But this time without the carrier bag."

"So what was in the bag?"

"Your guess, sunshine, is as good as mine."

"And what's your guess?"

"Money?"

"Why money?"

"Well, it's obvious, ain't it? Frankie Brigg works in the accounts department of this firm, the one he went to on Saturday. What do they do in an accounts department? They handle money, that's what they do. So I reckon this Frankie is syphoning off some dosh, in used fivers, in all probability. He stuffs the money in the bottom drawer of his desk. Now, Monday to Friday, his offices are full of people, so he can't just walk out the door with the cash in a bag. But on Saturday there's hardly anyone there. So in he goes, shoves the loot in a bag and out he walks. Dead easy."

It sounded implausible. It also sounded better than any idea I could come up with. That was mainly because I couldn't come up with any ideas at all. The more I thought about it, the less sense it made. Frankie Brigg goes into work on a day when he shouldn't be there, he cheerily breezes past the security man at the gate, wanders into his empty office, stuffs some illicit money into a carrier bag – and then does *what*? Goes to Kilburn to hand it over to Simon Baron?

"So when Frankie left the building in Kilburn, what did he do next?"

"He got on the tube."

"And where did he go?"

"The possibilities are endless."

"Meek!"

"What?"

"You did follow him, didn't you?"

"I saw him go into the underground station. You know, Kilburn Park…"

"And then?"

"I would have followed him. But, you know, it was getting late by then and…"

"Meek!"

"Look. It was Saturday."

"And?"

"Sat-ur-day," Meek said slowly, as though he thought I might be dim-witted. "Saturday aft-er-noon…"

"So?"

"Oh, for God's sake! Don't tell me you don't bleedin' know."

"Know what?"

"The World Cup!"

"Hell's Bells! You are not telling me you let a sodding football match come between you and an investigation, are you?"

"Come on," Meek whined. "Not just a football match. The World Cup. Some of the lads went round to my mate Eric's place to watch it on the telly. They got some beers in. 'Ere, did you see the way Geoff Hurst…?"

"No, I didn't," I replied tersely. "I was working at the time. On a job. That's what I do. When I'm on a job, I do the job. I don't interrupt the job to watch a football match."

"Yeah, well..."

"So, the end result of your little outing on Saturday is that we know that Frankie Brigg went to his office, we know he came out with a bag. And that's all that we know. Not much, is it?"

"He's on the fiddle," Meek said.

"Maybe he is. Maybe he isn't. Maybe he pinched some petty cash and then went to see his lady friend. Of course, we can't know that for sure because you decided that instead of following him, you'd get pissed and watch a football match."

"I followed him to Kilburn, didn't I? Like I said, he went into this building and when he came out he wasn't holding the bag. So maybe he paid off the bloke you was on about."

"Simon Baron? Maybe. But what's Frankie Brigg's connection with Simon Baron? Banning the bomb? Somehow I don't think so. Simon Baron didn't strike me as someone who's running a charity to bring about world peace. He struck me as a villain."

"There you are, then. What do people pay villains for? Guns, drugs, blue films."

"Blackmail?" I suggested.

"I could break into his house if you like."

"Simon Baron's house? I don't even know where he lives."

"Nah. Frankie Brigg's house. I could see if I can find any signs of what he's been buying from this Simon Baron bloke."

"Frankie Brigg's house is the same house as his wife's house," I reminded Meek.

"Yeah, so?"

"His wife is my client. Clients don't generally appreciate it if you break into their houses."

"Oh, yeah. I suppose."

"Anyway," I said, "whatever dodgy dealings Frankie Brigg might have as a side-line, that's not my problem. He could be nicking little old ladies' life savings to pay for gambling holidays in Monte Carlo and it still wouldn't be my problem. All I'm interested in is finding out if he's having it away with some glamorous housewife in East

Grinstead or Putney. That's all his wife wants to know, it's all I'm getting paid for, so anything else is none of my business."

17. An Awfully Big Bomb

I had forgotten all about Gregory O'Donnell. When he phoned my office later that morning, it took me a while to work out where I'd heard the name before. When I finally remembered, I arranged to meet him that evening in an Italian café in Soho. It was one of those cafés that smells of roasting coffee beans and is filled with the rumbling and hissing of steam from a huge, chromium-plated espresso machine. I arrived dead on the dot of six o'clock. He arrived about ten minutes later. He was wearing a cheap-looking wool-mix brown suit and he was carrying a rolled-up copy of The Catholic Herald in his left hand. When I saw him come in, I stood up and waved. He came across to my table, which was in a corner at the back of the café.

"Mr Kennick?" he said, hesitantly.

"Mr O'Donnell," I said, "take a seat." I snapped my fingers in the general direction of Gino, the café owner, who was busy at the counter. I stuck up two fingers in the "V" sign to mean "Bring me two coffees," though I realised the gesture risked being misinterpreted.

"Our mutual friend…" O'Donnell said, almost in a whisper, as though he was nervous of being overheard. He needn't have worried. With all the noise in the café, I could barely hear him myself and I was sitting two feet away.

"You are talking about Mr McJay," I said. I wasn't having all this "our mutual friend" malarkey. If we were going to talk about people, I wanted to be sure I knew who we were talking about. "Are you Catholic?"

"What? Oh, this!" He put the rolled-up copy of The Catholic Herald on the table. "No, that was… Mr McJay's idea. He said you'd need some way to recognise me. I thought The Times was more, well, traditional, but…well, too obvious, perhaps?"

Poor boy. He seemed to think he was in the spying game all of a sudden, just because McJay had arranged for us to meet and he'd told him to carry a newspaper so that I knew who he was. I had to give

McJay his due, the Catholic Herald wasn't a bad choice. It had the merit of being simultaneously dull and humorous.

Gino came across with our coffees: huge, frothy concoctions served in gigantic cups. As I sucked the froth off the top, I took my time to take a good, long look at the young man sitting opposite me. He was of average height and had average looks. His hair was dark brown with a floppy fringe that stopped just over his eyebrows. Although he was wearing a nondescript brown suit, he was far from monochrome. His shirt was pale blue and his tie was decorated with a pattern of gold and red flowers. I was surprised the Home Office permitted such garishness. His hair, I noticed, was long enough to overlap his collar. He was not the sort of person I would have expected to be the personal assistant to someone as blandly formal as Major Edward Willoughby-Styrt.

"You've known the Major long?" I asked.

"Oh, about a year. That's when I was moved to his department."

"You get on with him?"

"Oh, he's… a decent person."

Not a ringing endorsement, then.

"What exactly do you do in your department?"

"Well, I, um…"

"You are not at liberty to tell me."

He nodded.

"I already know you are involved with preparations for a nuclear attack," I said. "The Major himself told me you liaise with the military and various monitoring groups, the ROC and so on. Actually, I first met the Major during one of those exercises down in Bully Fen. Apparently, central London will be burnt to a cinder when the bomb goes off. But with a bit of luck Hackney will escape relatively unscathed."

O'Donnell sniggered into his coffee.

"What? Did I say something funny?"

"It's just that you may have a slightly optimistic view of what an H-bomb detonation actually involves."

"Really? To be honest, it's not something I've thought much about. The Major led me to believe that your lot were preparing for a ten-megaton bomb dropped on Marble Arch, thereby taking out everywhere from Bond Street to Buckingham Palace but leaving the rural vistas of Hackney relatively unscathed."

"Well, that is possible, of course. But not very likely. You see, the effects of the blast would be different depending on the altitude – I mean, whether the thing was detonated close to ground level or at some distance up in the air. If the latter, then the radius of immediate destruction would be greater. A one-megaton air-detonated bomb would cause massive destruction within a ten mile radius!"

"*One* megaton?" I said. "I didn't think the Ruskies worked with bombs much less than ten megatons."

He gave me the sort of sadly condescending look that my old maths teacher used to give me when I handed in my homework. "Ten megatons is an awfully big bomb, Mr Kennick."

"So one megaton is the practical limit?"

"I didn't say that. The Soviets are quite capable of deploying anything up to fifty megatons. And, of course, there is no reason to suppose they will only drop a single bomb."

I pictured Warden Featherglade running up and down the street blowing his whistle while the Women's Institute served tea and fairy cakes in the marquee. It was good to know that Britain was prepared for the worst. I distinctly recalled the Major assuring me that Hackney wouldn't fare too badly after a ten megaton bomb dropped on central London. Maybe I'd misunderstood. Or maybe he had been taking advantage of my trusting nature. Or maybe he made a habit of lying to the lower orders – just as he'd lied about his wife's non-existent garden gnomes?

"Anyway," I said, "if the bomb ever hits, I don't suppose we'll know anything about it."

"Unless we should happen to be outside the area of immediate destruction, of course. The effects of radiation are, in some ways, more worrying than the effects of the initial blast."

I wasn't in the mood to explore that rib-tickling subject any further. "The documents that went missing," I said. "Did they have anything to do with…?"

He looked uneasy again. "I'm afraid I…"

"You are not at liberty to say what was in the documents."

"That's right."

I changed tack. "It was you who noticed that some documents had gone missing?"

He made a sort of "Mmm" noise that was muffled by the froth of his coffee. I took it to mean "yes".

"Tell me about that."

He wiped some froth off his top lip. "What do you want to know?"

"Are you sure the documents were ever in Major Willough…" I saw the sudden look of panic on his face. His eyes went wide. He looked as though he was about to faint. I think he was worried that enemy agents might be seated at tables nearby, probably listening in on our conversation using miniaturised microphones. I decided to play along. In a theatrical whisper, I said: "Are you sure, the documents were in his briefcase when he left the office on the Friday afternoon?"

"They were there. He asked me to get them. I got them. I put them in a folder. A cardboard folder. An orange cardboard folder. We use orange folders for documents and green folders for correspondence."

"I don't think the colours matter," I said. "Just as long as you are sure the documents were there."

"I handed him the folder and he put it in his attaché case."

"What time would that have been?"

"About half past two. I have lunch from one to two. After lunch I got the documents for him. It must have taken me about half an hour to do that. So, yes, about half-past two, I'd say."

"And between putting the documents into his briefcase..."

"His attaché case," O'Donnell corrected. I didn't know what the difference was between a briefcase and an attaché case but I took his word for it.

"Between putting the documents in his attaché case and driving home for the weekend, where was the attaché case?"

"The Major had it."

"In his office, you mean? Could he have left it there, gone out somewhere later in the afternoon, maybe, leaving the case unattended?"

"No, not in his office. He went home. It was a Friday. He has a cottage in the country, you see. And on Fridays he drives there."

"But before he went home, could he have left the case…?"

"He went home as soon as I gave him the case."

"At half-past two?"

"Yes."

"Isn't that a bit early?"

"Not really. He usual leaves early on Fridays."

"So nobody could have tampered with the brief… with the attaché case, before the Major left?"

"No. Anyway, the case was locked."

I smiled. How anyone could place any faith in those silly little locks baffled me.

"Did anyone else know the documents were in the case?"

He thought about that a moment. "I don't think so. Well, Pat, I suppose. She works in the document section. It was from Pat I got the documents. But I don't suppose she knew they were in the attaché case."

"Is there anyone else who might have seen the Major put them into his case?"

"I don't think so. Well, Mr Featherglade, of course. But I don't suppose he counts."

"Featherglade!" I nearly choked on my coffee-froth. He might have been referring to a different Featherglade, of course. But it is not a common name and I thought the odds against there being a different Featherglade in the Major's office were pretty good.

"You know Featherglade?" O'Donnell asked, hesitantly.

"Possibly," I said. "A shortish, plumpish sort of man. Grey moustache, round-glasses, a tendency to go red in the face?"

O'Donnell smiled. "That's him all right. Frank Featherglade. He's the office manager."

"Was he in the office when you gave the documents to the Major?"

"I can't be sure but I think so. He's always buzzing around somewhere. Keeping us all in order, as he says."

"You like him?"

"Do I *like* him? Who? Mr Featherglade? Well…" The long pause told me all I needed to know. "He's very efficient."

18. The Red E-Type

Some investigators hate following people. They feel self-conscious, like actors who get the shakes when they step out onto the stage. Following people doesn't bother me. I dawdle at a reasonable distance from the person I'm following and nobody ever notices.

There's no special trick to it. People walk along streets all the time and you never give them a second glance. No, that's not quite true. Maybe sometimes you do give people a second glance: you notice the fat man wearing tight trousers, you notice the blue-haired woman with the pink poodle, you notice the teenager combing his hair using the reflection in a plate-glass window. You notice anyone who looks or acts just a tiny bit unusual. Everyone else – ordinary, unremarkable people who are just going about their business – you see and you instantly forget.

The secret to following someone successfully is not to try too hard. If the person you are following makes eye contact and you immediately glance away, they'll think that's odd. If you hide in a doorway or behind a tree you will attract attention to yourself and they will know that you are up to something.

That's not what I do. I take my time. If I happen to turn down the same street as the person I'm following, well, there's nothing strange about that. People do it all the time. If we happen to look at one another, I smile slightly because that's what people do when they want to seem polite without being over-familiar. Nobody remembers me.

At least, they never had before. But that Monday night, it didn't work out as planned.

"Do I know you?"

"I beg your pardon?"

The man in the Harry Worth hat and glasses had turned to face me. It was the first time I'd seen Frankie Brigg close to. He looked pleasant enough: slim, slightly snub nosed, square chin. In spite of the dull, old-fashioned clothes, I could imagine that some women might find him attractive.

"Do I know you?" he repeated. "Have we met?"

"Hmm," I tried to give the impression that I was racking my brains to try to work out if we had or not. Eventually I said, "I don't think so. Unless it was at Fanny's party…" I didn't know anyone called Fanny and I hoped he didn't either.

He decided to come straight to the point. "You are following me, aren't you?"

I looked startled. As though the idea that I would follow a strange man through the streets of Soho struck me as astonishing. "Following you?" I said.

It was a warm, bright evening and we were standing outside a coffee shop in a street whose name I can't recall, somewhere between Carnaby Street and Oxford Street. I couldn't think of any legitimate reason why I would be down there at that time on a Monday evening.

Frankie Brigg said nothing for a few moments. He just stood there looking me in the eye. Then he said, "Are you going to the Dragon?"

I had no idea what the Dragon was but I guessed it might be a pub. If so, that would provide me with an excellent excuse for taking the same route that Frankie had taken. It was the end of the working day and it seemed reasonable that both of us might happen to be making our way to the pub for an after-work pint.

"As a matter of fact," I said, "yes, I am. You?"

"Yes. I bit your head off just now, didn't I? Let me apologise. It's been a hard day."

"Not to worry," I said. "It's the heat. I've been stuck in a stuffy office all day myself."

"London always seems stuffy in summer," he said. "Let me buy you a drink."

This was not quite the way it was supposed to go. When you are following a subject, you are supposed to do so discreetly. You are not supposed to go to pubs and buy one another drinks. But I was in a situation where I had only two choices: I could go to the pub or I could make my excuses and leave. So I went to the pub.

Just as we got there Frankie took off his hat and, to my astonishment, he folded it in half and shoved it into one of the pockets of his overcoat. I had been working on the assumption that the hat was a proper trilby – the sort you might buy in Lock's of St. James's. A proper trilby is not a foldable item. The hat that Frankie Brigg had been wearing was not the sort of hat that Lock's would sell. It was more the sort of thing you might get from a department store or a mail-order catalogue. It was a cheap, flimsy affair that was no doubt advertised as "convenient and stylish headwear for the fashion-conscious young man". He looked better without it. Then he took off his glasses, folded up the legs and stuck them in the breast pocket of his jacket. Either he didn't really need them or else he was so vain about his appearance that he didn't care. Without the hat and glasses, he looked totally different. The hat and glasses made him look fuddy-duddy, middle-aged before his time. He ran his fingers through his hair, causing a small fringe to flop down over his forehead.

"Well, you got to let your hair down sometimes, ain't you?" he said. "Some people say that when I have my hair like this, it makes me look like Crispian St. Peters. What d'you think?"

"Maybe," I said, though I had no idea who Crispian St. Peters was or whether it was a good thing to look like him.

The pub was one of those nasty West End places that are all wood beams, with walls that used to be white but are now brown from cigarette smoke, and with beer prices that bring tears to your eyes. It was Frankie Brigg who bought the beer and my eyes watered in sympathy.

He asked me what I do for a living. "Insurance," I said, thinking that sounded vague enough to mean almost anything and dull enough that he wouldn't want to know any more about it. "And you?"

"Import/Export," he replied. That sounded about as vague as my answer but I was more persistent than he was.

"What sort of thing?" I said. "Gold? Silver? Diamonds?"

"I wish!" He smiled. Now that he'd taken off the Harry Worth hat and coat, I realised that he wasn't bad looking. There were plenty of women who'd have gone weak at the knees at that boyish smile with the two dimples in the cheeks. "Nah. It's medical stuff."

"Medical?" I said the word as though it was the most exciting job description I'd ever come across. "You're a doctor, then?"

"Me? No. Inventory. On the phone half the time, filling out forms the rest of the time."

"You married?" It was a leading question. I already knew the answer.

He smiled. "What do you think?"

His answer surprised me. I'd expected a simple "Yes", "No" or "It's none of your bloody business." But "What do you think?" What kind of answer is that?

"I just wondered if you were a free agent. Come and go as you please."

"I have lots of interests," he said. "I'm often out in the evenings. You?"

Every question I asked, he turned into a question to me. The question I really wanted to ask was, "Who are you bonking on Mondays and Thursdays and where does she live?" But I didn't think he'd answer that question either.

There were a couple of lads on the far side of the bar who were drunkenly singing the World Cup Willie song. That gave me the chance to change the subject. "Did you watch the game on Satur…?"

I was interrupted by a man standing behind me. Which was probably just as well since I know nothing about football and if Frankie had asked me a question about the World Cup, I'd have been stumped.

"'Ey, Frankie!" the man said, "Didn't think you'd be in tonight, boy. So 'ow's things, then?"

He was a tall man with fair, curly hair. He was wearing a double-breasted suit, expensive-looking, carrying a briefcase in one hand and a pint of beer in the other.

"Pete!" Frankie Brigg said. "Yeah, I was working late tonight. Nearly didn't make it. Pull up a seat. This is…"

I hadn't told him my name and I had no intention of doing so. "Harry," I said. That was becoming my alias of choice. Blame Harry Worth.

"Pleased to meet you, Harry." I noticed that Pete didn't look at all pleased to meet me. Quite the reverse, in fact. "Work with Frankie, do you?"

"I…"

Frankie interrupted before I had a chance to reply. "We bumped into one another. On the way here."

"Bumped into one another?" Pete echoed.

"Yeah. You know how it is. Hey, you'll never guess. Harry's in the same business as you."

My heart sank. I knew nothing about insurance. Even less than I knew about football. I hoped he wasn't going to ask me anything technical.

"Yes," I said, "but let's not talk about work."

So we sat and we talked about the weather and the cost of living and the wage freeze and the war in Vietnam and the hit parade and hairstyles and all kinds of other things that I can no longer remember. It was meaningless natter and none of us were really interested in it. I got the feeling that if I hadn't been there, Frankie and Pete would have been talking about other things and that maybe those other things might be more germane to my investigation. But as long as I was there, they avoided those other things like the plague.

We'd been chatting away for about fifteen minutes or so when this Pete bloke starts to get antsy: shifting in his seat, looking at his watch, drumming his fingers on the table top. And Frankie Brigg notices this; and he and Pete exchange glances and even though they don't say a word, it's obvious that they've come to some sort of decision. And then Frankie looks at me and he says, "Me and Pete are going on to a place." And I say, "Oh, yeah?" trying not to sound too interested but just a bit curious. "You know," he says. And I shrug because, of course, I have no idea what he's on about. "Earls Court," Pete adds. And Frankie says, "You know," again and gives a nervous little snigger like a schoolboy who's just said a naughty word.

"Earls Court?" I say, and I glance at my watch. "I'm working tomorrow. I thought I'd get back home. Make an early night of it."

"You ever been?" Frankie goes on. "To Earls Court?"

And I'm thinking to myself that he must be a bit simple because of course I've been to Earls Court and quite a dump of a place it is. But I'm also thinking to myself that when he asks me if I've been to Earl's Court, he really means have I been to a certain place in Earls Court. I get the feeling he's sizing me up. Working out if I know "the scene" or whatever they call it. So I nod and try to look all-knowing and worldly-wise and I say, "Yes. I've been. And, well, I mean, I'd like to come tonight but…"

Then Pete, who's practically quivering with impatience by now, stands up and says, "Come on then, Frankie. We better be off."

Frankie stands too then but he decides to give me one last chance. "You sure you're not coming then, Harry?"

And he nearly catches me out by calling me Harry because for a split-second I don't know why he called me that. But I recover quickly enough and I don't think he notices. So I say, "I'd love to come. But, you know…"

"Working?"

I nod. "Working."

"Shame."

"Yeah. But that's life."

So I give them a minute or so to leave the pub. And I'm wondering where they are off to in such a hurry. To meet the blonde girl I'd seen Frankie with in Kilburn the previous Monday? If so, who is she? Frankie's bit on the side? But if Frankie is going to meet the girl in Earls Court, he'd hardly take his mate with him, would he? Then again, maybe that's the "in" thing these days. Three in a bed. Four if they'd taken me along too. Maybe they had a squat in Earls Court: free love, drugs and an unlimited supply of Mateus Rosé. Frankie Brigg didn't look the sort for that kind of thing. Then again, who does?

Or maybe they are going to a hostess club? The sort of club where good-looking young women seated alone at tables are all waiting to be pleasant to men – for a price. Or maybe Earls Court has more innocent pastimes on offer? Literary societies? Theatre clubs? Nuclear disarmament meetings? The only way to find out for sure, of course, is to follow them.

I keep a tweed flat cap in my pocket. I don't like tweed flat caps. They don't suit me. I put it on. It wasn't much of a disguise, but it was the best I could do at short notice. I realised that I was doing exactly the same thing that Frankie Brigg had done less than half an hour earlier only in reverse. He'd taken off his hat, I'd put mine on. The thought occurred to me that maybe Frankie Brigg had been trying to disguise himself too. Maybe the cheap trilby hat and National Health specs were his disguise.

Down at the end of the street I could see Frankie Brigg and Pete walking off towards the tube station. I followed. I hadn't gone ten yards when there was a squeal of brakes in the road alongside me.

The squeal caught my attention. The car caught my attention even more. It was a bright red E-Type Jaguar. One of those models with a roof that can be put up or down depending on the weather. The weather was good and the roof was down. Sitting at the wheel was a young man with collar-length auburn hair. He was wearing a cream blazer, a yellow polo-neck sweater and a self-satisfied smile that revealed his pearly-white teeth to good effect.

"Jump in!" he shouted. It was the fashionable young man I'd spoken to the previous Thursday night in Kilburn – Simon Baron. The proprietor of a dubious enterprise called "Baron's Fine Living".

"Thanks for the offer," I said, "but I'll walk. I'm only going to the tube."

"Jump in!" he repeated. The smile faded from his face.

"Sorry. I don't get into cars with strange men. My mother warned me not to."

"I thought you wanted to see me," he said.

"Why did you think that?"

"You've been asking around."

Who had told him, I wondered? The woman from the Christian Evangelical publishing house with offices next to Baron's? Or Irena Duvere, the clairvoyant with rooms on the ground floor?

"I'm not interested in you, Mr Baron."

"You know my name, Mr Kennick."

"It's on your door. And you know my name, Mr Baron."

"It's on *your* door."

I didn't like the sound of that. It gave me the impression that he'd been following me. In my business, when any following needs to be done, I prefer to be the person doing it.

"Put bluntly, Mr Kennick, if you are interested in me, or in my business, I'd prefer it if you told me to my face. Make an appointment. What I'm not so keen on is having you scurrying around behind my back. Poking your nose into things that don't concern you. It's bad for business."

"Knickknacks?" I said.

"Come again?"

"I am told that your business involves the buying and selling of knickknacks."

"You see, you *have* been poking your nose into things."

"It happened to come up in conversation. Personally, I am not interested in knickknacks. Or in people who buy and sell them."

"On the whole," he said, "it would be better if it stayed that way." There was a sudden roar of the engine and the Jag accelerated away down the street at a speed that was in clear contravention of the Road Traffic Act of 1956 as well as several local bylaws. Had there been a police constable to hand, it would have been my duty to bring that fact to his attention. As there wasn't, I just grumbled to myself about long-haired louts with too much money and no respect for their elders.

The truth is, I couldn't have cared less about Simon Baron or his knickknacks. He was the sort of person who, when I write formal reports for clients, I refer to as being "tangential to my enquiries". All I was interested in was Frankie Brigg's whereabouts on Monday and Thursday nights. On Thursday nights, it seemed that his whereabouts overlapped with Simon Baron's whereabouts. That was the beginning and the end of my interest in Simon Baron. Nobody was paying me to investigate Baron so, as far as I was concerned, he could be the biggest villain in Kilburn and it still would be no concern of mine.

Baron had got the wrong end of the stick. He'd heard I'd been snooping around in the building where he had an office and he assumed that he must be the subject of my enquiries. Which meant for sure that he had something to hide. Even so, I still wasn't interested. Maybe I should have been. If only for my own safety.

Anyway, the upshot of my unplanned discussion with Simon Baron was that I had lost sight of Frankie Brigg. I could have gone to Earl's Court and asked around but that would have been a waste of my time and it would only have drawn even more attention to the fact that I was following him.

That was twice in a row that I'd lost track of Frankie Brigg. Maybe I wasn't as good at tailing people as I'd always thought.

19. A Man Of The Utmost Integrity

It was a muggy Tuesday morning and I was in a bad mood. I'm in a bad mood most mornings but Tuesdays are my speciality. On Monday there is a hope that a bright new week will be more sparklingly exciting than the previous week. By Tuesday, that hope has faded and all I have to look forward to is another tedious, dull, frustrating week just like all the others. The phone rang.

"Yes!" I snapped.

"I do hope I didn't call at an inconvenient moment."

It was McJay.

"Every moment you call is inconvenient," I said. "What do you want?"

He wanted to know how the investigation was progressing. I told him it wasn't progressing at all. This was mainly due to the fact that my client, Major Edward Willoughby-Styrt, was an arrogant fool who seemed to consider it beneath his dignity to provide me with any relevant, accurate or useful information which might assist my investigation. In short, he was a pain in the arse and a liar. My other client, a certain Turlough McJay, was an even bigger pain in the arse and an even bigger liar. But I didn't mention that.

"You went to the Major's country cottage, I believe," McJay oozed. "I thought you might have telephoned to make me au fait with developments."

"There are no developments to make you 'au fait' with," I said.

"You have no leads? Really, Mr Kennick, you disappoint me."

"As far as I can see, there are only three people who had the opportunity to nick those documents. One is the Major's assistant, Gregory O'Donnell, but frankly he is too much of a spineless drip to have done anything that needed that much initiative. Then there's a bloke called Featherglade, who is a pompous twat but who is also, in all probability, as honest as the day is long. And finally, of course, there's the Major himself."

McJay gave one of his cream-curdling chuckles. "Major Willoughby-Styrt? Come, come, my dear fellow, you really cannot allow your imagination to run riot. The Major is a man of the utmost integrity. He is a personal friend of Lord Mountbatten."

"Maybe he's a man of integrity and maybe he isn't," I said. "I won't know for sure until I've done a bit of digging around."

"Digging around? No, no, quite out of the question, old chap. Should your investigations lead you in that direction, I would strongly suggest that you find some other direction, and that most speedily."

"You mean, if he's guilty, I frame someone else?"

"In any transaction there are two parties – at *least* two parties – involved. The missing documents in this case must have been passed *from* someone *to* someone. I should take a closer look at this Featherglade fellow if I were you. Not forgetting the other chap, of course."

"What other chap?"

"The young man who came to such an untimely end at the Civil Defence exercise in Bully Fen. I presume your investigations are focussing very strongly upon that sad event."

"You may presume whatever you like. Whereas, speaking for myself, I presume that's a police matter. I try not to get involved in police matters. They can get messy."

"A police matter? Certainly not. Why would the police be interested? It was a clear-cut case of accidental death."

I laughed. "A knife between the fourth and fifth ribs. A funny sort of accident that would be. Come on, I know the form. Post-mortem, inquest, the police interview the witnesses, they check the whereabouts and motives of any family, friends and enemies of the deceased. I'm surprised the police haven't been round to interview me. Since I was at the scene of the crime, more or less, at the time it happened."

"Along with many hundreds of other people, it should be said. No, no, the police have no interest in the demise of Corporal Welbridge. His death was accidental. The man fell. Landed badly on a piece of jagged metal. Most unfortunate, but there you are."

"That's not what you told me."

"What I told you is strictly between the two of us, old chap. What I am attempting to convey to you is that you are most unlikely to run into any, what shall I say? 'interference' from the police should you choose, as I would strongly recommend that you do choose, to conduct your own investigation."

"You sneaky bugger," I said. "Are your lot buying off the police?"

"What a dreadful suggestion! I am shocked that you have such a low opinion of our organisation."

"OK," I said, "so you want me to find out if anyone had it in for Corporal Welbridge. Before I can do that, I need to know a bit about him."

I was expecting to be told things like his regiment and service record. But it turned out he wasn't a regular soldier. Corporal Nathan Welbridge had, until his recent fatal "accident", worked in a "sports and fitness" shop in Soho which is another way of saying a sex shop. He'd done his national service a few years back and climbed to the dizzying rank of private. More recently, just to while away his weekends, he'd volunteered for Civil Defence exercises. They let him pretend to be a Corporal.

I finished my chat with McJay and I was just about to leave the office when Meek showed up.

"Where you off to?"

"Soho," I said.

"What's in Soho?"

"Tailoring shops, Italian delicatessens, striptease clubs, blue cinemas…"

"Yeah, yeah, I know what's in Soho. I mean, why are you going there?"

"To try to find out some things about a dead man."

"I know plenty of people in Soho. If I come with you I can help out."

"Not this time," I said. "I've got to go somewhere else first. Somewhere where it'd be better if I was on my own."

"Yeah? Like where?"

"Birdcage Walk," I said.

He looked none the wiser. "I'll look after the office while you're out. You never know, maybe Kitty Brigg will drop by?" He gave a rasping laugh that didn't convey the sort of cool, professional interest in my client that I would have wished.

20. Birdcage Walk

Whitehall is a part of London that was designed to make the likes of you and me feel insignificant. Lined with squat, blocky buildings in the Victorian style, it is the heart of Government, the heart of the Civil Service and was, not so long ago, the heart of the British Empire.

Whitehall stretches from Trafalgar Square to Chelsea but the important part is the area around Parliament Square. Here you will find everything from the Ministry of Defence to the Cabinet Office – a vast ants' nest of busy civil servants scurrying around in an effort to advance or frustrate the wishes of the Prime Minister and his lackeys. Unless he happens to be taking time away in his country house "Chequers" or on holiday in the Scilly Isles, the Prime Minister himself can be found just around the corner from the Cabinet Office in a gloomy little house in Downing Street.

There are, in fact, numerous small streets that lead off from the main thoroughfare of Whitehall and it took me a while to find the one I was looking for. According to McJay, Major Edward Willoughby-Styrt worked in a department called The Civil Defence Liaison Unit in Birdcage Walk. To be honest, I'm not sure if Birdcage Walk is really in Whitehall at all. It's more like "Whitehall Garden Suburbs". It took me a good half an hour to get there, having started out from Admiralty Arch and walked at a brisk pace along Horse Guard's Parade. I could have got there faster by cutting across St James's Park (and not stopping off to buy an ice cream on the way) but I didn't know that at the time.

I was in no hurry anyway. I'd caught the tube into town, got off at Piccadilly Circus at around ten to four and, having time on my hands, I dawdled through Trafalgar Square to watch the tourists feeding the pigeons. Then I walked up to Admiralty Arch, expecting to find Birdcage Walk more or less adjacent, which it wasn't.

They say that when you are lost in London you should ask a policeman. It's a firm principle of my life that I never ask a policeman for anything so I asked a tourist instead. He was a pleasant young man with a camera over his shoulder and a street map in his hand. It was the street map that drew me to him. I asked him if he could tell me where Birdcage Walk was and he gave every indication of wanting to help me to the full extent of his capabilities. Since, however, he only spoke Japanese, his capabilities didn't extend very far. I resorted to pointing at his map and smiling. He smiled in return, nodded a few times, said something in Japanese and handed over the map. Map-reading has never been one of my most highly developed skills but after turning the map around a few times and looking at it from different angles, I eventually worked out that Birdcage Walk was to the south-west of where I was standing and, having handed the map back to my Japanese friend, that's the direction in which I went.

From its name, I assumed that Birdcage Walk would be a quaint little mews terrace. Far from it! It is a broad, tree-shaded avenue which, on one side, is lined by solid stone buildings with high doorways and balustraded rooftops and, on the other side, by the leafy vistas of St James's Park. It was a nice location to have an office, I thought. If I ever win the pools, maybe I'll relocate there. Since I don't actually do the pools, however, that doesn't seem likely. What's more, I don't think many of the buildings on Birdcage Walk are on the market. Quite a few of them house the Whitehall overspill – second-ranking Government Offices, shady outposts of the security agencies, branches of the Civil Service that most of our elected politicians probably don't even know exist. I'm not sure who the other buildings in Birdcage Walk belong to. Wealthy businessmen, maybe? The type who do dodgy deals in oil, gold and diamonds. Then again, maybe I'm just being cynical. Maybe there are some blissful family homes there: mother, father, a couple of kids, a cook or two and a singing nanny. I don't think I'd fit in. I've got the wrong accent and I don't know how to eat peas from the back of my fork.

By the time I'd found the address I was looking for I'd finished my ice cream, so I sat on a bench in the park at a convenient position for observing the building at the other side of the road. It was around five o'clock by that time. I'd bought the evening newspaper at a shop just off Trafalgar Square and I unfolded it to read the news of the day. I glanced at the headlines. Some people had been drowned in Cornwall. Some people had been shot in Texas. The situation in China was causing concern, the situation in Russia was growing worse, the war in Vietnam was much as it always was. I crumpled up the newspaper and threw it into a nearby wastebin.

Across the road, nothing much was happening. People were strolling past, enjoying the late afternoon sunshine. I half-closed my eyes and pretended to doze. Someone on a motorbike drew up outside the building that I was watching; he parked, took something from a box on the back of the bike, went into the building and, a few minutes later, came out again empty handed. Delivering documents, maybe? I wondered how many documents were shuttled between various Government departments on a daily basis and how often they went missing?

A few minutes later, a skinny, youngish, red-headed girl came out of the building. She was doing up her overcoat. Shortly afterwards, two men came out, talking and laughing. One was carrying a brief-case. I didn't recognise them. Then, five minutes after that someone I did recognise came out. I reached into the waste paper bin, retrieved the crumpled newspaper, straightened it out and put it in front of my face in the hope that it made it look as though I was reading it. The person I'd recognised was Gregory O'Donnell, the man I'd met in a café in Soho. It hadn't occurred to me that he worked here. That was an oversight on my part. Since he was Major Willoughby-Styrt's assistant and the building contained Major Willoughby-Styrt's office, naturally his assistant would also work there.

When I next glanced over the top of my newspaper, O'Donnell had moved away down the street. Probably going to catch a tube or a bus to take him home, wherever that might be. I was no longer interested in O'Donnell. So I stayed where I was and kept watching the building. A few more people came out, alone or in small groups. And then finally I saw the person I was waiting for.

I stood up, glanced left and right and then nipped across the road, only narrowly avoiding being mown down by a friendly London cabbie who gave vent to an impressive array of curses which he shouted through his wound-down window.

My quarry had already started off down the street but since he was moving at a sedate pace, it didn't take me long to catch up with him. He was wearing a long, navy-blue overcoat and a black bowler hat. In one hand he carried a briefcase. In the other hand he carried an umbrella. The day had been sunny and fine and there was barely a cloud in the sky. The umbrella was carried for effect rather than for any practical reason; with each step, the little man gave the umbrella a jaunty swing. Anyone seeing him in the street might have taken him to be someone of importance: a company director, perhaps, or a stockbroker, possibly even an MP. I put my hand on his shoulder, to attract his attention, which it certainly did. He gave an involuntary shudder then turned to look at me and recoiled with such force that for a split second I thought he might be about to have a heart attack. "My Goodness!" he sputtered. "You gave me quite a start, Mr Kennick."

I apologised profusely and added, "If you could spare me a few minutes, Mr Featherglade, there are some matters you might be able to help me with."

*

We sat on a bench in the shade of a big tree in St James's Park, far enough away from his offices (I hoped) to avoid any unplanned encounters with Featherglade's workmates. I particularly didn't want to bump into Major Willoughby-Styrt. Even though I was doing a job for him, I wasn't sure where his job ended and McJay's job began. If he'd seen me talking to Featherglade, it would have complicated matters.

"How are you progressing?" he asked. "With your investigation, I mean?"

I wasn't sure how much Featherglade knew about my investigation. The Major had fobbed him off with some story that I was "from the Ministry", whatever that might mean, but maybe that was just for public consumption. O'Donnell had told me that Featherglade was the office manager so I assumed he knew more than he was letting on to.

"I'm making progress," I said. "But slowly."

"Ah."

I looked at my watch. It was twenty-past five. "Does the department shut this time every day?"

He sat up straight and fingered his moustache with obvious pride. "Five o'clock on the dot. With military precision, you might say. Though I leave a little later since it is I who lock the office."

"Really?" I said with an air of abject humility as though I could hardly believe my luck to be in the presence of the man who locked the office. "I didn't notice the Major leaving."

"The Major?"

"Leaving the office. I didn't see him."

"You were watching?" he said, suspiciously.

"I was sitting on a bench, reading a newspaper."

"Ah. The Major didn't leave at five o'clock because he wasn't in his office. He went to lunch, you see."

"It must have been a long lunch."

"Things have to be discussed."

"Who did he go to lunch with?"

Featherglade's moustache bristled. "I could not possibly reveal that, I'm afraid."

I sighed to show how disappointed I was. The fact of the matter is that I wasn't interested in who the Major had gone to lunch with. He could have taken Leonid Ilyich Brezhnev for a slap-up meal at the Dorchester for all I cared.

"Does the Major often take long lunches?" I asked.

"Occasionally. Did you want to speak to him?"

It was time to get to the point. "No," I said, "I want to speak to you."

"Me!" He looked flustered. It made me wonder if he had any secrets he didn't want me looking into. "Really, Mr Kennick, I can't imagine what you might want to speak to me about. I really know nothing about…" He came to an abrupt halt. He stroked his moustache nervously. "I know you are assisting the Major with some matters. But really, I think it is the Major himself to whom you should be speaking, not me."

"Were you in the Army?" I asked.

"The Army?"

"In The War, I mean?" I hoped he could hear the capital "T" and the capital "W". I wouldn't want him to think I meant just any old war.

"In The War?" he said, slowly, giving the impression that for the moment he couldn't quite recall what he'd done. "As a matter of fact, I was in the Navy."

That threw me. I know very little about the Navy. They whiz around in ships and occasionally fire big guns. That's about the full sum of my knowledge. Then there are the Royal Marines. They can be tough bastards. They have their own special operations units, men trained to do the dirty, dangerous work – the ruthless bastards that go in and get the nasty jobs done. Frank Featherglade didn't look that sort to me. For one thing, he was a bit on the short side, and for another thing, he was a bit on the plump side. He looked more like a suburban bank manager than a trained killer. Then again, The War was over twenty years ago, People can change a lot in twenty years.

"Did you see action?" I said.

"Some."

"Hand to hand?"

"What do you mean?"

"Unarmed combat. Or armed combat, come to that? With a knife, say. Do they train people in hand-to-hand fighting in the Navy?"

He gave me one of his self-important schoolteacher looks, glancing at me over the rims of his glasses as though he was about to chastise me for gross impertinence and order me to write out one hundred lines: "I must not be cheeky to my superiors."

"I fail to see why you are so interested in my naval career," he said, at last.

A little boy came past, kicking a football. The football came hurtling towards my legs. I kicked it back towards the child who gurgled something between mouthfuls of the ice lolly he was sucking.

"Did you ever kill anyone?" I asked. "At close quarters, I mean?"

He laughed. "Mr Kennick," he said, "you seem to have formed an erroneous impression. My experience of armed combat is negligible. I was certainly trained to use a knife but only to dice vegetables and remove the bone from a joint of pork. I was a cook, Mr Kennick. My War was singularly lacking in excitement. Now, if there is nothing more pertinent with which I may help you, I really must be getting home. My wife will be wondering where on earth I've got to."

"You have a place in town?"

"Good Heavens, no! My salary barely covers the cost of running our house in Little Froomly. I certainly could not afford to rent another place in town. No, Mr Kennick, just like thousands of other people, I am a commuter. I catch a train into town in the morning and another train to take me home in the evening."

My conversation with Mr Featherglade had, it seemed to me, yielded little in the way of useful information. I decided to have one final go at getting something out of him. "What do you know about Burlington?" I said.

He glowered at me. "You asked me that once before."

"No, I didn't."

"I beg your pardon but I must contradict you. I remember very clearly. When I showed you around the ROC post last Saturday, you asked me where it was and I told you I didn't know."

"You are wrong. I didn't mention Burlington."

Featherglade opened his mouth to say something, then closed it again. Then he opened it again. And once more he closed it. He looked like a goldfish in a bowl.

"You can't remember, can you?" I said. "You are not sure if it was Burlington or Turnstile I asked you about. Why is that? Because Burlington and Turnstile are one and the same thing. And you know exactly what that thing is."

"Mr Kennick," – with some effort, he stopped doing goldfish impressions and tried to look as though my question hadn't caught him by surprise – "even if I knew what it was, I could not tell you. I would, however, advise you not to enquire further into the matter."

"I have to enquire, Mr Featherglade. That's my business."

"So it may be. My business is to keep to myself matters which I am not at liberty to reveal."

In fact, he had revealed more than he realised. He said that I had previously asked him where Burlington was. I hadn't. At the ROC post, I had only asked about Turnstile. And I hadn't asked *where* it was. I'd asked *what* it was. Now I knew that Burlington or Turnstile or whatever the current name might be, wasn't a *thing*, it was a *place.*

Featherglade stood up. My interview was clearly at an end. "There is one thing I will tell you, however," he said, "since it has already been made more public than we would have wished. If the details of Turnstile were ever revealed, it would be of far greater consequence – far more damaging to our country, I should say – than the revelations relating to RSG-6. And Heaven knows, that was close to catastrophic. Good evening, Mr Kennick."

Featherglade tipped his bowler hat to me and walked away as briskly as his bulk permitted, swinging his umbrella as he went. He cut a ridiculous figure in some respects: a silly, pompous little man with a tedious, commonplace job for which he compensated by adopting an air of superiority and arrogance. He was one of those dull but decent people who just get on with their lives and try to make the most of it. Or so I assumed. But, after all, what did I know about him? During "The War" he had been a navy cook, now he worked as an office manager in an obscure offshoot of the Home Office. He held a senior position in a Royal Observer Corps monitoring post and he was also a volunteer Warden – someone who would help out in the event of a nuclear attack. He commuted between London and a little village near Watford every day and he had a wife who was waiting for him at home. All things considered, he was an ordinary, unlikeable, public-spirited man who did his best to serve his country.

Might he have stolen the documents from the Major's attaché case? I didn't think so. Could he have murdered Corporal Welbridge? That didn't seem likely. And yet somebody had done both those things. And if suspicion fell on Featherglade, what then?

If suspicion fell on Featherglade I would, in all probability, receive new instructions. From McJay, perhaps? Or from Becker? Or from someone else whose name I would never know? Ultimately, I wouldn't need to know who made the decision. All I would need to know is that a decision had been made. I would be told that harmless, self-important Frank Featherglade has become an annoyance. One that has to be dealt with. Once and for all. He would have to be got rid of.

And if I received orders to get rid of him, would I follow those orders?

Of course I would. That's my job. It's what I'm good at.

21. Rendezvous In Berwick Street

Soho at that time on a summer's evening is one of the most beautiful places on God's Earth: the air is warm and still, the shadows are lengthening, the light is a pale gold, the birds are twittering in the branches in St James's Park and the boys are lining up against the railings in Piccadilly Circus. On a twenty minute walk through London, you get to see more of life than you'd see in twenty years out in the suburbs.

By day, when you walk through the streets of Soho you'll smell roasted coffee, freshly-baked bread and the mingled smells of French cheeses, Italian salamis and Polish sausages. As evening comes, the coffee shops and bakeries and delicatessens shut their doors and, little by little, the night-shift takes over. Night is my time. I feel at home there.

McJay had given me the name of the "sports and fitness" shop in Soho where Nathan Welbridge had worked. It was called The Blue Canary. I didn't know the significance of the canary but the meaning of "blue" was pretty obvious. McJay hadn't given me an address. He didn't know it, he said, but relied on my boundless ingenuity to find it. From the tone of his voice, I got the impression that people of McJay's class don't soil themselves with tawdry places like Soho. Or, anyway, that's what they'd like you to think.

I decided to take a stroll down to Berwick Street to have a short chat with a tailor there by the name of Sol. If you want to know anything about the seedier goings on in that part of town, Sol's the man to ask. But I hadn't gone there to ask the address of The Blue Canary for the simple reason that I don't like Sol to know too much about my business activities. Sol's a lovely bloke but he can't keep his mouth shut. That's handy for me when I want to know what other people are getting up to. But it's also handy for other people when they want to know what I'm getting up to.

"Sol," I said, "you ever hear of a place called Turnstile?"

"What sort of a place would that be?"

Sol was smoking a cigar while hunched over a worktable and drawing chalk lines all over a big piece of brown pinstripe worsted. It's a thing that tailors do mid-way between unrolling a piece of cloth and turning it into a suit.

"I don't know what sort of place it is. I just know the name. I thought to myself, who do I know who knows just about every place there is to know in London?"

"A taxi driver you should ask," Sol said. "Ask a taxi driver where a nightclub is and he'll take you there."

"I tried asking a taxi driver," I said. "I went to the taxi rank in Liverpool Street."

"You talk to Joe?"

"I talked to half a dozen cab drivers. None of them had heard of the Turnstile."

Sol gave me a pitying look. "You should have talked to Joe. Joe's the best cab driver in London. If anyone knows where this place is, Joe will know."

"I'm relying on you, Sol. When I drew a blank with the cab drivers, I asked myself, who'd know more about the highways and byways of London than my dear friend, Sol?"

He blew a stream of rank smoke through his nostrils (whatever he was smoking, it wasn't a fine old Havana) and appraised me with a professional eye. "You're not wearing the suit I made you."

"I save it for special occasions."

"I make you a suit and you save it for special occasions? You should get me to make you another suit for ordinary occasions. That thing you're wearing, I wouldn't be seen dead in. What is it, polyester?"

I didn't take his bait. If I let him get me talking about suits, before I knew it he'd be measuring my inside leg and giving me a special deal on a bulk order.

"You've never failed me before, Sol. You know I rely on you. Sometimes I think I'd never solve any case if it wasn't for the help I get from you."

Sol smiled and brushed away some flakes of ash that had fallen from his cigar onto the brown worsted. "There's some truth in what you say but I'll need a few more clues. One word is all you've given me. You get better clues with The Times crossword."

"OK," I said. "Here's another one. Subterfuge."

"Subterfuge? What's that supposed to mean?"

It was another one of the names on the list that the Major had run through when we'd had our meeting in the marquee at Bully Fen.

"Subterfuge sounds like the sort of name they'd give one of those places in Mayfair. A dancing club maybe?"

"How about Burlington?" I said. "There's some connection between Burlington, Subterfuge and Turnstile. But I don't know what it is."

Sol stopped making chalk marks on the cloth. He looked up at me. He took a good, long drag on his cigar, removed the cigar from his mouth and blew out a stream of smoke with an air of deep significance. "Ah," he said, "so that's what you are talking about. You said it was in London. That's why I couldn't make head or tail of it."

"You think they are out of London?"

"Of course they are out of London. Only it's not a 'they', it's an 'it'. Burlington, Subterfuge and Turnstile are three names for the same thing. But if you're thinking of looking for it, forget it. You'll never see it."

"Why not?"

"It's underground."

"A basement club?"

"Are you the detective or am I? No, it's not a basement club. Why are you asking about it if you don't even know what it is?"

"It's a job I'm working on. I can't go into the details."

"You are doing a job that involves Turnstile? Ha! That I find hard to believe."

"Save the witticisms, Sol. Just tell me what it is."

"Oh, I'll tell you. I can tell you while I do the measurements."

"What measurements?"

"For the suit you said you wanted."

"I never said…!"

"You are not telling me that you plan to go on wearing this shabby piece of rubbish." He rubbed the right lapel of my jacket between his thumb and forefinger with an expression of disgust on his face. "And in public, too!"

"I'll buy a suit from you," I said.

He took the measuring tape from around his neck.

"But not today," I added. "Today I'm working."

Sol slung the tape around his neck again and wiped his hands on a piece of white cloth that was lying on his workbench. He clearly considered that he had been soiled by touching the lapel of my polyester jacket.

"Since it's you," he said, "I'll tell you. Though, a man of your intellect, I'm surprised you don't already know. Turnstile…" Sol stopped mid-sentence and looked around the shop. It was empty. He looked around the shop again. It was still empty. The only sound to be heard was the sound that a tailor's shears make when they cut through cloth. That was Sol's cutter, Charlie, working in the back room. "For your information," Sol continued in a whisper, "Turnstile is top secret."

"Really?" I said. "So how come a tailor in Berwick Street knows all about it?"

"My brother's wife's cousin's daughter works there. In the kitchen."

"So are you going to tell me what it is and where it is or not?"

"I can do better than that. I can draw you a map." So he did.

22. SOHO AT NIGHT

"Lovely to see you, pet." Maggie had a smile that could break your heart. She also had other desirable features but they cost extra.

"Good to see you too," I said. "You look as stunning as ever."

"And you," she said, "look almost as worn out as your suit."

"You're just flattering me," I said.

She gave a throaty laugh that made cigarette smoke puff out of her nostrils in little clouds. "Are you just fishing for compliments or have you come for witty conversation and a bit of slap-and-tickle?"

"I'll settle for the conversation," I said. "At my time of life, slap-and-tickle might be more than my heart can stand."

"More than you wallet can stand too, dear." She laughed again. That's what I love about Maggie. No matter how bad things get, she somehow manages to get through life with her sense of humour intact.

"Let me get you a gin and tonic," I said.

She held out her glass. "Make it a double and don't bother about the tonic."

We were in one of those charmless, dark, nondescript pubs somewhere in a warren of grubby little streets at the heart of Soho. They sold watery beer and watered-down spirits. The clientele was mostly made up of small-time crooks, the kind that sell dodgy French perfumes made from horse piss and cheap scent, or who fleece foreign tourists with the Find-The-Lady trick on the Tottenham Court Road. And then there are the girls. The girls know most of what's going on under the grubby surface of respectable London. They know the pimps, the thieves, the pornographers and the drug-dealers. They also know the people who use the services of the pimps, the thieves, the pornographers and the drug-dealers. If they wanted to, they could ruin the careers of some very important people and bring down the Government as an added bonus. But (as Maggie once told me), who'd take the word of a tart?

I sat there chatting with Maggie for a while but God alone knows what we talked about. Everything and nothing. Maggie told me a funny story about a well-known film actor who'd asked to be handcuffed to a bed but he was so drunk that he fell asleep as soon as the cuffs were on. When he woke up he found he was in the Savoy Hotel and the Archbishop of Canterbury wanted to know why he was in his bed. All the girls have stories like that. They always happen to one of the other girls but nobody's every quite sure which one. Then I asked her about The Blue Canary. She knew the place. It was down a dead-end street not far from the Windmill Theatre.

"I didn't think that was your sort of thing," she said.

"What sort of thing would that be?"

"You know." She made a face as though she'd eaten a sour lemon. "Continental."

I didn't know what that meant exactly but I guessed it was porno magazines and films of the sort that the British Board of Film Censors would not deem to be suitable for a family audience.

"Kinky," she added.

I thought I had a pretty rich imagination. Leather, whips and chains sprung to my mind. My imagination wasn't as rich as I'd supposed. Maggie gave me a few hints about the kind of goods that were available at The Blue Canary. I'd heard about stuff like that but I'd never seen it and I didn't want to. It was the sort of stuff that could get you a hefty jail sentence. If you got caught.

"They won't get caught," Maggie said. "They pay all the right people. You know who I mean."

I could make an educated guess. The seedier side of Soho only exists thanks to the protection of certain people. Some of those people wear suits, some wear uniforms. In theory, the ones wearing the uniforms are supposed to be on the other side of the fence from the ones wearing suits. But the reality is a bit different.

"He got killed, I heard," Maggie said. "One of the blokes who worked there."

"Nathan Welbridge. Yes, he did."

"Was that his name? Everyone called him Nate. He was a sadistic bastard, that's what I heard, anyhow."

Some men who hang around Soho take advantage of the girls: threaten them, blackmail them, use them, and not always gently. I wondered if Nate was one of that sort.

"He beat up the girls?" I said.

Maggie gave that smoky laugh of hers again. "Almost right," she said. "Except he wasn't interested in girls."

23. THE BLUE CANARY

The Blue Canary looked like any one of the dozens of blue magazine and film shops in the grimier backwaters of Soho. Its name was flashing on and off in neon, its windows were painted black and there were billboards on either side of the door proclaiming "Adults Only XXX", "Nude Studies" and "Continental Books".

I took a deep breath, pulled down the brim of my hat and went in, first through the outer door and then through the multi-coloured bead curtains hanging over a second door-shaped gap. I was wearing a long overcoat and a trilby hat. I looked like a typical customer. I found myself in a narrow room, about ten feet long by six feet wide. On either side of the room, from floor to ceiling, there were shelves filled with magazines. There was just one customer in the shop at the time (a man wearing a long overcoat and trilby hat). He was browsing through the magazines as though looking for the financial pages. At the far end of the shop there was a counter on which stood a till. A man in a denim shirt was leaning on the counter, smoking a cigarette and reading a paperback book. The book was a Hammond Innes adventure story. Not the sort of book they sold in The Blue Canary.

The man at the counter glanced up as I entered, said "Evening," and carried on reading the book. His face was familiar, but I couldn't quite place him. He looked different out of uniform.

"Browse all you like," he said, without looking up from his book. "But don't crumple the pages."

It was the accent that gave him away. I had a mate once who came from the valleys of South Wales. He had the same accent. My mate's name was Bill but everyone called him Taffy. That's what they called the man behind the counter too. I'd seen him before – twice. On the first occasion, he'd been holding the rear end of a stretcher on which reclined a woman who'd been rescued from beneath a fallen telegraph pole. The man holding the front of the stretcher had been "Corporal" Nathan Welbridge.

The second time I'd seen him he'd been sitting on a pile of rubble outside a ruined sweetshop. Nurse Briony Barrington had been sitting next to him, comforting him. It had been Taffy who had found Nathan Welbridge's body.

I glanced at the magazines. They weren't my cup of tea. There were grainy photographs of well-proportioned women throwing beachballs at one another, and middle-aged women dressed as schoolgirls, complete with gym-slips and ponytails. Towards the top shelves there were a few magazines in sealed plastic bags. They appeared to be of the "sexy housewife" variety. The cover models looked like the same women who'd been dressed as schoolgirls, only this time they'd slipped into frilly black nighties. There were magazines catering to other tastes too: cowboys, sailors, athletic young men wearing posing pouches that were only just on the right side of the law.

I moved towards the counter.

"Excuse me," I said.

Taffy looked up from his book. "What?"

"Have you got anything a bit more 'Continental'?"

He took a few seconds before he answered. Those few seconds gave him time to give me the once-over. He was trying to decide if I was a copper and, if I was, whether or not I was one that The Blue Canary was already doing business with. I passed muster.

"What sort you after?" he said. He said it almost in a whisper. Maybe he didn't want the other customer to hear.

"What sort have you got?" I asked.

"You tell me what you are looking for and I'll tell you if we got it."

It was then that I noticed that there was another of those beaded curtains just behind the counter. I noticed them because they rattled. Taffy turned and said something to the man who emerged through the curtains. I took advantage of the opportunity to leave the shop. I hoped that the man who'd come through the bead curtains hadn't recognised me, because I had recognised him. He was a tall man with long, straggly hair, a beaky nose and protruding teeth. He was wearing a ratty looking coat with what looked like the fur of a mangy dog sticking out around the edges. The last time I'd seen him, he'd been in the company of a chap who bore a striking resemblance to Mick McManus the wrestler.

24. Sex And Bombs

"No, I never heard of it."

Meek was sitting with his feet up on my desk. Straker was curled up in his lap having a quick forty winks. The fly was buzzing around the room without a care in the world. I'd been telling Meek about Turnstile. I'd even shown him the map that Sol had drawn. It was scrawled in blue pencil on a sheet of tracing paper. Don't ask me why Sol had used a blue pencil and tracing paper. It's the sort of thing that tailors do.

"You haven't heard of it," I said," because it's top secret."

Meek yawned. "Then how come you know about it?"

"Long story."

"Why's it called Turnstile?"

"Your guess is as good as mine. It's also called Burlington, Stockwell and Subterfuge."

"I know Stockwell," Meek said. "There's a pub there called The Three Boars…"

"Not the same Stockwell," I said. "Burlington, Stockwell, Subterfuge and Turnstile are codenames for the same thing. All this here," I pointed to the map that Sol had drawn, "is underground. It's huge. Twenty, thirty, forty acres maybe."

"Underground?" Meek yawned again. He'd been doing a job down the West End the night before. Security at a private club is what he'd told me. Which probably meant he'd been working as a bouncer in a strip joint.

"It's somewhere near Bath. When the bombs drop that's where all the bigwigs will go. The Government, the Army. Maybe the Royal Family? While the rest of us will be left to take our chances."

"And what's this got to do with you?"

"It's got something to do with a job I'm doing."

"The bomb job?"

"The stolen documents job."

"Same thing. I mean, you're doing a job for a bloke who's getting ready for the day when people like me and you will get blown to smithereens and all the important people scurry off to live in the lap of luxury in this place…"

"Turnstile," I said.

"Yeah." Meek yawned again. I wondered how much he'd had to drink the night before and how much, if any, sleep he'd had since. "And this place turns out to be a secret underground city. Right?"

"In all important details, yes."

"Then that proves it."

"Proves what?"

"The job you're doing. It's something to do with bombs. Atom bombs."

"Hydrogen bombs," I corrected.

"What's the difference?"

"Hydrogen bombs go off with a bigger bang."

"There you are, then. That's what this job is all about."

"The stolen documents were lists of toilet rolls," I said.

"Yeah, well, I suppose even secret underground cities have toilets."

"Of course, there may have been other documents too. The Major hasn't gone out of his way to entrust me with too many details about Turnstile."

"How did you find out about it?"

"The Major told me," I said. "The first time we met. In Bully Fen. He told me the name. But he wouldn't tell me what it was."

"Probably because it's top secret?"

"Probably. Only…"

"What?"

"Well, if it's so damned top secret, how come my tailor knows about it?"

Meek guffawed.

"What's so funny?" I said.

"'My tailor', the man says! Since when have you had your own tailor?"

Meek was looking scathingly at my suit through bleary eyes. It was a crumpled suit, off-the-peg, a cheap polyester mix that didn't fit in all the places it was supposed to fit. "This isn't my only suit," I said. "I have a better one. Bespoke."

"You should wear it."

"In fact, the reason I went to see my tailor was to get measured for another suit."

Meek yawned again. "Oh yeah?"

"Or maybe a couple of suits. I haven't made my mind up yet."

"I'll believe it when I see it!"

Meek picked up the mug that was sitting next to his feet on my desk and took a long drink of tea. It was stone cold. A skin had formed on the surface. That was because the tea was left over from the day before. Meek didn't seem to notice. "So you are saying that your tailor told you all about a place that's so top secret that some bloke playing soldiers down in Hackney got bumped off because of it?"

I shrugged.

"And you believe him?" Meek began to laugh but the laughing hurt his head so he stopped.

"My tailor happens to be very well informed. He has lots of contacts."

"He's spinning you a line. Making it up. They have a keen sense of humour, your tailoring profession."

There was a brief pause while Straker stretched out his paws and Meek groaned. During the pause, I thought over what Meek had just said.

"The man in Hackney. The one who got killed," I said. "We don't know that he was connected with the documents that were stolen from the Major."

"Course we do," said Meek. "Stands to reason. Bound to be."

I was about to say "It could be a coincidence," but I didn't really believe that. Coincidences like that don't happen.

"So what's the connection, then?" I said.

"You tell me," said Meek. He was having trouble keeping his eyes open. He rested one elbow on the desk and then he rested his chin in the palm of his hand. "After all, you're the detective. I'm just the trainee."

I didn't like the sound of that. Meek was a mate and I sometimes gave him a few quid for helping out. But a trainee detective? Definitely not. I would have to make that clear. But I didn't think now was the right time, mainly because Meek had slumped forward onto the desk and had begun to snore.

I made some tea and gave the cat a saucer of milk. To fill in the time, I looked at Sol's map again. It was a bit of a scrawl but it showed roughly where the living quarters were located, also the kitchen area, the main entrance lift and something called the Operations Room.

Maybe if I could find the location of Turnstile, I could go and have a look around. But I didn't fancy going all the way to Bath. And even if I did go and even if I managed to find the place, what would I do then? March up to the nearest guard and ask to be given a guided tour? Then again, maybe Meek was right. Maybe Turnstile was all a figment of Sol's imagination. Maybe there was no underground city that went on for tens of acres. Maybe, in fact, I'd be better forgetting all about the bomb job and concentrating on the infidelity job which, to be frank, was more my cup of tea.

Then again, how much had I managed to find out about Frankie Brigg and his illicit affairs? The answer was: not much. The previous Thursday he'd gone to see some flash-dressing bloke called Simon Baron who ran a dodgy business in Kilburn. On the Saturday, when Meek had followed him, Frankie Brigg had gone to his office, came out with something in a plastic bag and taken it to Simon Baron. Then on Monday, when I'd been tailing him, he'd met an accountant friend of his in an overpriced pub down the West End and the two of them had gone on to somewhere in Earls Court. And then – surprise, surprise! – who should I just happen to bump into, driving past in his shiny red Jag, but Simon Baron? Maybe Brigg was doing some dodgy business deals with Baron? And maybe he was drinking away his profits with his accountant friend in a seedy Earls Court nightclub? Maybe, maybe, maybe…

So there I was. Two jobs on the go and not a bloody thing to do except twiddle my thumbs and listen to Meek snoring.

It occurred to me that it might be useful to find out a bit more about Simon Baron.

25. Knuckledusters And Knickknacks

Someone called my name. I shouldn't have turned to see who it was. But I did turn and that's when he slugged me. A hefty uppercut to the jaw.

Random acts of violence can happen to anyone. You can go walking down a quiet, tree-lined street, looking for a cosy little pub in which to while away a pleasant half-hour when, out of the blue, some nasty little teenage thug belts you around the head and steals your wallet. But this was not a random act of violence, it wasn't a teenage thug and he didn't want my wallet. He'd been watching me. I didn't notice he'd been watching me because I'd been too busy watching someone else. Or, at least, waiting for an opportunity to watch someone else. Frankie Brigg, that's who'd I'd been waiting for. But that's not who slugged me.

I was back in Kilburn, standing in the doorway opposite the dilapidated Victorian building where Frankie Brigg had gone the previous Thursday. Why he'd gone there was still a mystery. He'd told his wife he was going to a meeting of something called The International Peace Collective (North London Branch). But unless Simon Baron was secretly bringing about world peace under cover of running a business called Baron's Fine Living, The International Peace Collective was notable by its absence. Which meant that Frankie had been telling his wife some prime porkies and it was my job to find out what he was really getting up to.

It was Thursday evening and I'd arrived at the location in Kilburn at about twenty to eight. After half an hour of watching, I'd seen nothing of any interest. Nobody had entered the building and nobody had left. There wasn't a light on in Baron's office – or in any room on the first floor. Then again it wasn't a dark evening. Not as dark as the previous Thursday had been. On that occasion the sky had been covered with thick grey clouds from which vast quantities of rain had descended, much of which had gone down the back of my collar and trickled its way downwards towards my shoes. I'd brought an umbrella this time but the weather wasn't playing my game. It was one of those dry, warm, bright, silvery evenings that you sometimes get towards the end of summer just when you are least expecting them. Which may have explained why there wasn't a light on in Baron's office. There was a light on in a room on the ground floor, though. Irena Duvere's room. I wondered what she was up to? Reading the future in a deck of cards? Communing with the spirits of the dead? Or did she have some other occupation as a side-line? Call me a cynic, but I wasn't sure I really believed everything she'd told me.

If there was a light on in Irena Duvere's room, that meant there should be a light on in Baron's office too – if someone was in there. Didn't it? Or maybe a room on the ground floor was darker than one on the floor above it? Or, then again, maybe tonight's meeting of the International Peace Collective (North London Branch) was due to start later than the one that had taken place the previous Thursday? Or maybe I was just wasting my time? Just because Frankie Brigg had come to see Baron last week didn't mean that he would come again this week.

At ten past eight a light went on – in a room on the first floor. I couldn't be sure but I thought it was Baron's office. I thought I saw someone moving around inside. I stepped out of the doorway to take a closer look. That was when I got socked on the chin.

In films, when the hero gets socked on the chin, the screen goes black, someone strums a few relaxing notes on a harp and then the victim wakes up somewhere else. That's not how it happens in real life. I've been socked on the chin more often than I like to admit and only once did everything go black. That was in a boxing match with Corporal 'Hammerfist' Malloy. Boxing is not one of my great talents. But I was in the Army and I didn't have any say in the matter. Malloy punched me on the side of the head, everything went black. Nobody played the harp but I woke up next morning with a headache you could boil eggs on.

Luckily the person who socked me on the chin in Kilburn was not in the same league as Hammerfist Malloy. The punch rattled my teeth a bit but I didn't black out. I did get annoyed, however. So annoyed that before I really knew what I was doing I'd swung my umbrella in the general direction of my attacker. In case you've never used an umbrella as an offensive weapon, here's a handy tip: you should hold it by the pointed end so that you can get a good swing of the heavy end – namely, the handle. It helps if the umbrella has a solid wooden handle. Mine had. When it made contact with my assailant's skull, I heard a satisfying *thwack*. Then I heard laughter: high, nasal, braying laughter. In between the snorting laughs, I heard the words: "He... hit you... with his... umbrella!" And then more laughter.

The laughing man was wearing a knee-length coat with moth-eaten furry edges. I recognised him at once. He was one of the men I'd seen leaving the building shortly after Frankie Brigg and the blonde girl had left it, the previous Thursday. I'd also seen him behind the counter of a dodgy Soho shop called The Blue Canary. He was tall, willowy, had long, scruffy hair, protruding teeth and a beaky nose. When I had described the moth-eaten coat to Meek, he'd told me it was called an Afghan Coat and was all the rage among the trendy set who bought their "gear" from "boutiques" in the environs of Carnaby Street. Now I had a chance to get a better look at him, the man reminded me of Cardew Robinson. I don't know if you've seen Cardew Robinson. He's a comedian. A bit out of fashion, now. I saw him once in a film called "Fun at St Fanny's". I was abroad at the time. In the jungle. If you've never seen a Cardew Robinson film in the jungle, don't worry, you haven't missed much. I can't remember what the film was about. It was a bit like St Trinian's, I think, but without Sabrina. You'll have seen Sabrina, I suppose? She's doesn't say much but with a figure like that she doesn't need to. Anyway, even though Sabrina wasn't in the film, Cardew Robinson was and he looked the spitting image of the bloke standing on the street in front of me. Except, of course, Cardew Robinson wouldn't have been seen dead in a mouldy old Afghan coat.

The other man, the one who'd hit me, had staggered back against the wall of a building and was holding one hand to the side of his head. He was the other man I'd seen the previous Thursday – the one who looked like the wrestler Mick McManus. Seen close up, he looked even more like Mick McManus. I knew that he couldn't be the real Mick McManus though because, if he had been, the uppercut to the jaw that he'd just given me would have done a lot more damage.

"What did you hit me, for?" I said. The uppercut might not have been as debilitating as he'd hoped for but it didn't improve my sunny good humour.

"I thought you had a gun," Mick McManus said.

"A gun?" I said.

"It was an umbrella," the tall willowy one snorted. He clearly found the incident hilarious.

"I know it's an umbrella," I said. "I brought it in case it rained."

"It could have been a gun," said Mick McManus.

"It isn't," I said, for the sake of absolute clarity.

"I can see that now," said Mick McManus. "I'm sorry I thumped you."

"So am I," I said.

"Yeah well," he added, "mistakes happen."

There was an awkward pause due to the fact that we'd run out of scintillating repartee. The tall, willowy bloke who looked like Cardew Robinson broke the silence with the observation that it wasn't raining and according to the BBC weather forecast, it was set fine for tomorrow too. I glared at him. Mick McManus glared at him. The mutual glaring gave us a shared sense that we were both the innocent victims of an uncaring world that was stuffed full of idiots like the tall, willowy bloke who looked like Cardew Robinson. The next thing that happened was that Mick McManus apologised again, even more fulsomely than before.

"I just meant to attract your attention," he said.

"You succeeded," I replied.

"Only," he added (he'd pushed himself away from the wall by this time and had stopped rubbing his head, which made me wish I'd put a bit more force into the umbrella-swing), "only, see, we was wanting to have a word."

"Not us," Cardew added. "The boss."

I may not be the quickest thinker in the business. Ask me to multiply 7 by 23 and you'll be waiting a very long time for an answer. Even so, it took me less than five seconds to figure out who "the boss" was.

"Simon Baron wants to see me?"

"Yeah," said Mick.

"That's right," Cardew added.

I was starting to get the impression that Simon Baron was taking an unhealthy interest in me. On Monday night he'd followed me in that flash Jag of his. And now he'd set his two goons to keep an eye out for me. Which made me wonder why he had thought that I might happen to be visiting the less fashionable end of Kilburn tonight. Had he been tailing me? He had a damn' cheek if he had!

"Did he tell you to work me over first?" I asked.

Mick McManus gave a broad grin from which, I noticed, two front teeth were missing. Maybe he'd had a previous encounter with someone who knew how to swing an umbrella better than I did? "No hard feelings, I hope," he said. "That was an honest mistake, mate. Still, no harm done, 'ey?"

I smiled as much as my aching jaw would permit. "And if I decide not to accept Simon Baron's invitation?"

Cardew gave a braying laugh. Mick and I stared him into silence.

"I'd suggest that you accept his invitation," Mick said.

I got the strong feeling that if I refused, Mick McManus would insist. Now that he knew I wasn't carrying a gun, his next punch might be one of the "everything goes black" variety. I don't like violence. Especially when it's done to me. So when Mick pushed open the door to the building I followed him inside, with Cardew trailing close behind.

"Watch your step," Mick said. That was nice of him, I thought. Less than five minutes earlier he'd socked me on the jaw. Now he was warning me to watch my step in case I accidentally hurt myself. Maybe he was getting to like me?

Once on the first floor we walked past the darkened windows of Room 2A (the Christian Evangelical publishers; I wondered if Reverend Pillingham had ever turned up to collect the five hundred inspirational tracts for the Sierra Leonean mission?) and stopped in front of Room 2B which had a frosted-glass window set into the upper part of the door through which a dim, yellowish light was shining.

Cardew opened the door and Mick pushed me inside. Room 2B was, in all important details, almost identical to Room 2A. Its walls were painted in the same, sickly pale green with a similar ratio of damp patches and flaking paint. Just like Room 2A it had a lightbulb in a dusty shade dangling from a frayed wire in the middle of the ceiling. It had a creaky wooden floor and two windows facing onto the street (I'd have to remember that fact when I next tried working out the total number of rooms in the building by counting the windows). There was an oblong desk made of metal and plywood. There was a calendar on the wall showing a very large blonde woman in a very small bikini. The main difference between Room 2A and Room 2B was that the former was piled high with Bibles, prayer books and devotional tracts whereas the latter, the room in which I was now standing, was totally devoid of them. I don't think Room 2A had the calendar either.

"Not a religious person, then?" I said, just to make conversation.

He raised an imperious eyebrow. Oh, I forgot to mention, the other difference between Room 2A and Room 2B was that Room 2A was occupied by a little, grey-haired woman whereas Room 2B was, at that moment, occupied by Simon Baron. The little grey-haired woman was entirely harmless; Simon Baron wasn't. It was Baron who was sitting at the other side of the desk and raising his imperious eyebrow in my direction.

"Sit," Baron said.

"That's very kind of you." I looked around to see what sitting options were open to me. There were two chairs in the room. Baron was in one of them – an expensive-looking armchair upholstered in red leather. The only other one was a hard wooden chair on my side of the desk. I was thinking of making a humorous remark about the lack of a chaise-longue but when I saw Mick McManus scowling at me I decided to keep the jokes for another occasion.

I sat.

"You keep turning up, Mr Kennick," Baron said.

He was smartly dressed, in a dandyish sort of way: single-breasted suit (pale blue), silk shirt (pale yellow), rakishly-tied cravat (multi-coloured). The suit looked classy, well-cut, more Savile Row than Berwick Street. Where did a man like Baron get that kind of money, I wondered? He was young – mid-twenties, I'd say – but, not, I thought, from a wealthy background. His accent gave him away. He was trying to sound posher than he really was but every once in a while the East End showed through.

"There's something that keeps drawing me back," I said. "You know how it is. For some people it's Paris in the springtime. For me, it's Kilburn after dark."

He smiled. "You're an intelligent man, Mr Kennick." I assumed he was trying to flatter me. I'm not easily flattered so I didn't bother to smile. "You must realise that someone like me is not likely to take kindly to being… I was going to say 'spied on' but let's not jump to conclusions. Let's just say I don't like someone like you taking an interest in me."

"I promise you, Mr Baron," I said, "I'm not in the slightest bit interested in you."

"Then why do you keep turning up?"

"I've got nothing else to do. I was thinking of going to Monte Carlo for the season but I couldn't find anyone to feed the cat. So Kilburn it is."

Cardew sniggered. It was a penetrating, nasal, braying sort of snigger. Baron didn't join in the fun. He slammed his fist on the desktop and frowned. Cardew got the message. Within a second, all was silence.

"I know your business," Baron said. "I know what you do. You spy on people. I don't like being spied on, Mr Kennick. I don't like it at all."

"I can understand that, but…"

"Who's employing you?"

"I can't tell you. Client confidentiality, you know."

Baron stood up. He went to one of the windows and looked out, then he turned around and took a few steps towards me. It was all part of an act. The silence, the walking about, standing over me, looking down at me. It was intended to intimidate me. I stood up. I faced Baron, looked him in the eye. He hadn't told me I could stand. He knew it was a challenge. He was wondering whether to tell me to sit down again, wondering whether to tell his pet thugs to make me sit down. It was a touch-and-go moment. I was playing a dangerous game. But so was he. We both knew it. Eventually, he came to the conclusion that it wasn't worth the hassle of provoking me. Not here, not now. Though maybe in some other place at some other time…?

"I'm a businessman, Mr Kennick," he said. "Just like in your business, there are certain things I need to keep confidential. You can understand that." He went back around to the other side of his desk and sat in his fancy red leather chair. After a few moments I sat too. Mick McManus had taken up a position a foot or two behind me. I saw him slide his right hand into his jacket pocket. I caught a silvery glint. Knuckledusters. So he was prepared to play dirty. That didn't surprise me. Especially not after the belting I'd given him with my umbrella.

"What kind of business are you in, Mr Baron?" I asked.

"Fine living, Mr Kennick. It's what young people demand these days."

"Young people?"

"Younger than you," he said. "No offence meant, but…"

"What sort of fine living do young people demand these days, Mr Baron?"

He smiled. "There you go again. Trying to find out stuff that's no concern of yours. See, when you ask questions like that, I could end up thinking you are after my trade secrets. For all I know, you might be working for someone in the same business that I'm in. A competitor."

"Since I don't know what business you are in, I don't think that's likely."

Baron took a packet of cigarettes from an inside pocket of his jacket. "You smoke, Mr Kennick?"

"That isn't one of my vices."

He lit the cigarette with a gold lighter which was either a Dunhill or a very convincing fake. "What are your vices?" he asked.

"Whatever they are, I keep them to myself. Look, Mr Baron," I was starting to find his well-mannered menace irritating, "I've enjoyed our little chat but since I don't know anything about you and I have no desire to know anything about you, if you don't mind, I think I'll be getting along."

I stood up. Mick McManus shuffled closer to me. His right hand was in his jacket pocket, where he kept the knuckledusters.

"If you have no interest in me," said Baron, "just tell me why you keep turning up. I have a feeling that the pleasures of the night-time streets of Kilburn are not the only reason."

"OK, I'll tell you," I said. "I'm going to be absolutely honest with you. I'm on a job. Watching someone. But that someone isn't you."

"Who else is there?" he said. "There are my two associates, Mick," (Mick McManus smiled and for a second I wondered if he really was the wrestler or was the first name just a coincidence?) "and Terry." (The tall chap in the decaying Afghan coat sniggered. I thought the name Cardew suited him better but I can't be right all the time). "Apart from them," Baron went on, "there's no one in the building at this time of night. Except for the loony bint in the room downstairs." (Here, I assumed he was unchivalrously referring to Irena Duvere).

I shrugged. "I can't tell you anything about who I'm following or why," I said enigmatically.

"I happen to know that you are taking a keen interest in someone with whom I am acquainted."

"Oh yeah?" I gave him my wide-eyed, innocent look. He wasn't taken in.

"Someone called Frankie."

"Oh yeah?"

"I saw you a few days ago, if you remember?"

I screwed up my eyes a bit, struggling to drag out any memory of the event that might be lurking somewhere at the back of my skull. Eventually, I found it: "Oh, yeah!"

"You'd just come out of a pub. I happened to be driving past in my car."

"Nice car."

"Frankie had left that pub a few moments earlier."

"Oh, yeah?"

"Yeah. Coincidence, I thought."

"Yeah."

"If I was you, Mr Kennick, I wouldn't bother myself with Frankie Brigg. Know what I mean?"

"Not really."

"He could be trouble is what I mean. If you've got some kind of job that involves Frankie Brigg, my advice to you is get another job."

I thanked him for the advice. Then we exchanged a few more pleasantries: how warm it was for the time of year; the shocking price of a loaf of bread; how sad it would be if I happened to poke my nose in where it wasn't wanted and ended up breaking a few of my limbs down a dark alley one night. That kind of harmless, everyday banter. Then we said goodnight, Baron stood up, shook my hand and didn't even bother to try any funny stuff like wrenching my arm out of its socket or giving me a swift elbow to the solar plexus, which showed just how matey we'd become.

I headed out of the door followed closely by Mick and Cardew (It was no good, I couldn't think of him as Terry no matter how hard I tried – if anyone was born to be named Cardew, he was). There was a big cardboard box on the floor just by the door. I hadn't noticed it before. Well, cardboard boxes are not the sorts of things that grab my attention as a rule. There were, in fact, a few other cardboard boxes stacked against one wall. The boxes were about two-feet tall and three-feet wide. The one by the door had been opened. Through the flap, I could just about see what it contained: straw. The sort of straw that you either feed to cows or wrap fragile things in. Simon Baron didn't seem the sort of person to have a pet cow so I assumed that the box might contain something that could be easily damaged.

"Knickknacks?" I said.

"You what?" said Baron.

"I heard a rumour you traded in knickknacks. I have an eye for that sort of thing. It's possible to find some real bargains down Petticoat Lane. Statuettes. Shepherd girls traipsing through meadows with lambs, that kind of thing."

"Petticoat Lane?" Simon Baron made a grunting noise that might have been a laugh struggling to get out. "You are a tonic, Mr Kennick, you really are."

I was thinking of my conversation with Irena Duvere. She'd told me that people took boxes into and out of Baron's office late at night. She'd asked him what the boxes contained and he'd told her they were full of knickknacks. Simon Baron didn't strike me as the sort of person to run a business in cheap china ornaments. It wasn't his style. Which made me wonder what his business really was.

26. The Green Eye Of The Little Yellow God

There was a chap I knew once who specialised in dramatic and humorous monologues. He'd do "The Shooting Of Dan McGrew" and "The Lion and Albert". If he'd had a few drinks and there were no officers present, he did "The Ballad of Eskimo Nell" with added hand gestures. But the one he liked doing best was called "The Green Eye Of The Little Yellow God". It told the story of a one-eyed yellow idol to the north of Kathmandu and the fatal consequences for a certain Mad Carew when the Colonel's daughter took a fancy to the idol's eye. It's a heart-rending story but the thing is, it's obvious to everyone who hears the monologue that the idol is evil and the best thing Mad Carew could have done would have been to smash the bloody thing at the outset.

That's the way I felt about Meek's shepherdess statue. Whenever I came in, there it was, standing on my desk, glaring at me balefully with its little yellow eye. To be honest, I think the shepherdess's eyes were blue. But they were a particularly baleful shade of blue. It was a Friday morning and there was just me and Straker in the office. I had nothing to do other than the crossword and, to fill in the time, I started to think of interesting ways of destroying the statuette. I could smash it with a hammer, cut it into pieces with a hacksaw, throw it against the wall, dump it in a rubbish bin, chuck it into the Thames, give it away to a charity, tie it to a hydrogen balloon and send it up to the stratosphere…

Before I had a chance to put any of these plans into effect, the phone rang.

"Kennick Investigations. How may I help you?"

It was McJay. He was concerned about the lack of developments in my investigation. I told him his concern meant a lot to me. He thanked me. McJay's not good at irony. He wanted to know what I'd found out about Featherglade. I told him I'd discovered that Featherglade was a self-important, pompous little man but I didn't think he'd stolen any documents and I didn't think he'd killed Nathan Welbridge. In fact, I said, as far as I could tell, the prime suspect was Major Edward Willoughby-Styrt. McJay chuckled and reminded me that I had been with the Major at the time Welbridge had met his untimely end – which was true: the Major and I had been drinking warm beer in the refreshments tent. I told McJay that while that might give the Major an alibi for the murder, it didn't give him an alibi for nicking the secret documents. I thought of mentioning my visit to Nathan Welbridge's old workplace, The Blue Canary, but that would only have complicated matters. So I changed the subject: "What's RSG-6?" I said.

He harrumphed and wanted to know what my interest might be. I told that I'd had a tip-off that Turnstile and RSG-6 might have something to do with one another and that it would advance my investigation if I could find out more about it. He said he'd get some information sent to me. He added that on no account was I to attempt to visit Turnstile.

"So Turnstile is a place?" I said, innocently. For some reason, McJay was still trying to keep me in the dark about that. He didn't mind getting me to do his dirty work but he didn't think I was a proper person to know why I was doing it.

"It does not form a part of your investigation," he said.

"Is that a fact?" I replied, innocently, "Well, Major Teddy *does* form a part of my investigation. You know more about him than you've let on to me about. What else can you tell me about him?"

"Very little, I fear. It would be inappropriate, you see, for me to reveal private information. I'm sure you understand."

"Oh, absolutely," I said, thinking to myself that if only I'd had the right school tie, that wouldn't have been a problem.

"He will be away all weekend, of course," McJay added irrelevantly. "He invariably goes away to his cottage on Fridays. Leaving his London flat empty. Until he returns on Monday."

27. VANISHING ACT

By great good fortune, another job had come my way earlier in the week. It was one of those bread-and-butter, run-of-the-mill jobs that I wouldn't normally give a second thought to. A chap who ran a local florist's shop had noticed that his takings were down over the year even though business was booming or, possibly, blooming. He had two fulltime employees – a middle-aged man who was the shop manager and a young woman sales assistant – plus a woman who came in twice a week to do the cleaning. The shop owner suspected that one of his employees, or possibly the cleaner, had been dipping his or her fingers into the till but he didn't know which one of them it was. He'd taken to counting the money in the till at the start of the day and counting it again at the end of the day. He checked the money that came in and he checked the money that went out. Everything tallied with the books.

I went to watch the shop. I followed the employees as they came and went. By the end of the day I'd found the culprit. It was the shop manager. It was he who kept the accounts. When the owner went down to Covent Garden to buy in stock, the shop manager would enter the stock and the purchase costs in a ledger. A different ledger would be kept showing the income made from sales. The stock figures and the sales figures all tallied. As far as the shop owner could tell from looking at the records of stocks and accounts, everything was above board and everything balanced. But still his takings were down. It was a simple fiddle but one that was hard to spot because the owner never saw his manager doing the fiddling. He hadn't been dipping his fingers into the till, he'd just been putting the wrong numbers into the books: a bit less stock than they actually had went into the stock book, fewer sales than they actually made went into the sales book, so there would never be any discrepancies when the accounts were balanced.

The shop owner had known the shop manager for years. They were friends. A crooked friend is one of the hardest crooks to spot.

So how did I discover all this? Simple. I took the woman sales assistant to lunch. I came clean with her – told her I was a private investigator and that I was trying to find out who was stealing money from her boss. By that time, I'd already decided it must be the shop manager. I just didn't know how he was doing it. She told me.

As I said, it was a bread-and-butter, run-of-the-mill case and I wouldn't even bother mentioning it but for the fact that it gave me an interesting thought about Frankie Brigg. Specifically, about what Frankie Brigg had in the plastic bag when Meek had seen him leaving his workplace the previous Saturday. Frankie Brigg worked in accounts. So, just like the manager in the florists' shop, he could make things disappear. All he had to do was forget to put something into the stock book (or whatever they used in the company he worked for) and hey presto! it no longer existed.

Meek had seen Frankie Brigg take something in a bag from his company's offices and go down to Kilburn to see Simon Baron. If my guess was right, I had a feeling that whatever it was that Frankie Brigg had made disappear had found its way into that plastic bag. And that bag had ended up with Baron. All I had to do was to find out what was in the bag. And why Simon Baron might be interested in it. If I knew that, I might also discover why Simon Baron was so interested in me.

28. Spies For Peace

Later that afternoon, a motorbike courier brought me a foolscap manilla envelope. On the front of the envelope was typed my name along with the instruction "To Be Opened By The Recipient Only". On the back of the envelope was a small label on which had been typed: "Inaperçu Perfumiers of Covent Garden. Exclusive Aromas for Ladies and Gentlemen." Maybe McJay had been telling the truth. Maybe he really was moonlighting in the perfume business. When the courier left I gave the envelope a good, long sniff. It smelled of motorbike grease and traffic fumes. I put the kettle on, fed the cat, made a mug of tea, sat down, put my feet up on my desk and ripped open the envelope. It contained several grainy, photocopied pages. I was impressed that a perfume shop could afford a photocopier. There was clearly money to be made from scent.

There was a photograph on the first photocopied page. It showed a snowy landscape with some sort of small, squat, rectangular building. It could have been anything. The words printed on the cover gave me a clue. Looking as though they'd been stencilled, they said: "DANGER! OFFICIAL SECRET! RSG-6"

I flipped to the next page. This contained an introduction:

"This pamphlet is about a small group of people who have accepted thermonuclear war as a probability, and are consciously and carefully planning for it.

"They are above the Army, the Police, the Ministries or Civil Defence. They are based in fourteen secret headquarters, each ruled by a Regional Commissioner with absolute power over millions of people. In the whole of Britain only about 5000 men and women are involved; these chosen few are our shadow military government.

"Their headquarters are called Regional Seats of Government. Our story mainly concerns RSG-6, which will rule much of Southern England. The people in RSG-6 are professors, top civil servants, air marshals and policemen. They are quietly waiting for the day the bomb drops, for that will be the day they take over……."

The pamphlet went on to say that copies had been distributed in Britain and abroad, to politicians and the national press as well as to prominent figures such as Bertrand Russell and Albert Schweitzer. The pamphlet was dated "Good Friday 1963". Which meant it was more than three years old. At first, I assumed that the politicians who'd received a copy either hadn't bothered reading it or hadn't bothered making their views on it known to the general public. At any rate, if Bertrand Russell and Albert Schweitzer had read it and made their views known, I hadn't heard about them.

The pamphlet gave the locations and even the phone numbers of twelve secret Regional Seats of Government. It gave some very specific information about one of them – RSG-6 located in the village of Warren Row, near Reading. There was even a detailed map of the base and instructions on how to get into it.

"RSG-6 is not a centre for civil defence," said the pamphlet. "It is a centre for military government. It is the headquarters of the REGIONAL COMMISSIONER, who will have supreme power over the three million bodies in his region. In this headquarters the Regional Civil Defence Corps plays a minor and definitely subordinate part. RSG-6 is staffed by civil servants in the middle echelons, and by Service officers in the middle ranks."

The pamphlet claimed that the "smokescreen" around RSGs was intended to blind the citizens of Britain rather than to deceive our enemies. It ended with a plea to readers to reveal other Government secrets.

"Secrets are being kept from you because you may be a spy. Not for Russia, but for all people everywhere. Because you may believe you have the right to know what is being done about your future, in your name, at your expense, but without your consent.

"We are Spies for Peace. We have decided to publish an Official Secret. All we have is a voice. We have done what we can.

"You have a voice too. If you spread this story as widely and as quickly as you can, you will stop the authorities hiding it again.

"A SECRET HAS ESCAPED. Give it a good run before they catch it. Read it. Discuss it. Hand it round. Reprint it.

"THERE ARE THOUSANDS MORE SECRETS IN CAPTIVITY. This is not the only one we shall release.

"DO YOU KNOW AN OFFICIAL SECRET?"

I could see why McJay was worried. If releasing details of a poxy little local HQ like RSG-6 was an embarrassment to the Government, just think what the effect would be if people got to know about Turnstile. A vast underground city that extended over several acres and needed to be stocked with twelve thousand toilet rolls!

Could these people – these so-called Spies For Peace – have stolen the Major's documents? If McJay wanted me to do a 'special' job, would I find myself tracking down a peace protestor, rather than a Soviet agent? I hoped not. But it wasn't something I'd lose sleep over. It was a problem for another day.

That evening I went to the pub. Meek was there.

"You been fighting again, haven't you?" He shook his head disapprovingly. Just in case I was baffled by his astonishing deduction, he added, "You've got a bruise on your jaw."

"I know," I said. "I also know that the healing power of the aspirin is not all it's cracked up to be. I took a handful of them this morning and it still feels like someone's playing the Anvil Chorus in the back of my head."

"Anyway," he said, "I've had an idea."

I congratulated him. Then he told me what the idea was. That blonde girl, he said. I said, what blonde girl, as there have been so many blonde girls in Meek's squalid life that it's hard to keep track. The one Frankie Brigg went off with, he said, by which he meant the girl I'd seen him leave Simon Baron's building with on that rainy Thursday evening just over a week ago. I said, what about her? He said she might be Frankie Brigg's bit on the side. I informed Meek that the possibility had already occurred to me.

"I could tail her," he said. "I could go to Kilburn one evening. And if I see her leaving, with or without Frankie Brigg, I could follow her."

"She'd see you."

"I'd be discreet."

"Discreet? You?"

"Yes, me."

"And what if Simon Baron's thugs notice you? While you're being discreet, I mean."

"They won't. And even if they did, I'm not scared of them."

"Maybe you should be."

"Why? It's *you* they are interested in, not me."

He had a point. For reasons I hadn't fully understood, Simon Baron and his goons were taking an uncomfortable interest in me.

"So shall I follow her or not?"

"Up to you," I said.

Meek shrugged again. It was a surly sort of shrug. "So I'll follow her then."

"If you want."

"Fine."

The conversation ground to a halt after that so I got in a round of drinks.

"Here, take a look at this." I took the Spies For Peace pamphlet out of my inside jacket pocket and slid it across the table towards Meek. He took a quick look and said, "Oh, that lot! A proper lot of nutters, they are."

"You've heard of them?"

"Of course, I have. They was all over the newspapers a few years back."

According to Meek, back in April of '63, this had been a front page story. There'd been some kind of incident on the Aldermaston Peace march. A couple of thousand demonstrators had broken away from the march and tried to get inside one of the secret HQs. Whether or not they succeeded and whether or not the HQ was RSG-6 Meek couldn't remember. But he did remember that the incident had been provoked by a pamphlet – presumably the one I was holding in my hand – and there had been an almighty brouhaha about it.

"So how come you remember all that and I don't?" I said.

"I had a girlfriend at the time."

"Congratulations. I don't see the connection."

"She used to go on peace marches, demos, all that stuff. So I took an interest. It gave us something to talk about. A tasty little number, she was."

"Blonde?" I said.

"Platinum." A smirk of fond reminiscence flickered over his ugly face. "But not a natural."

Meek has always had a weakness for blondes. I was starting to have doubts about the wisdom of letting him go looking for the blonde girl I'd seen with Frankie Brigg. But, as it turned out, it was just as well that he did.

29. Breaking And Entering

Most Saturday evenings I like to go back to my flat, drink some whisky and read a book. That Saturday evening I had other things to do. I was going housebreaking. It was one of those squat, square Victorian houses with a few steps out the front leading up to a porch which was supported by Roman columns to give it a touch of class. It was on two levels – ground floor and first floor – and it was painted all in white, except for the door which was painted black. I don't much like white-painted houses, especially when I happen to be breaking into them. It was fully dark by this time and the nearest streetlight was about ten yards down the road. Even so, if anyone happened to look in my direction, they would have seen me silhouetted against the white walls. Between the porch and the pavement there was a small garden. The garden was separated from the pavement by a decorative wall with ornamental pilasters supporting a balustrade at waist-height. Midway down the ornamental wall, a wooden gate between two pillars opened onto a paved path that led up to the porch. A tall privet hedge was growing right behind the wall. The hedge had no doubt been added to provide some privacy so that passers-by wouldn't be able to see into the windows. It would also give me some privacy. Once I was in the garden, I'd be able to hide behind the hedge while I figured out the best way to get into the house.

It was all very swish, all very expensive-looking. I wondered how a man with a minor position in an obscure offshoot of the Home Office could afford a nice little pied-à-terre like this as well as an even nicer little "cottage" out in the rolling hills west of Watford. Major Edward Willoughby-Styrt was obviously doing pretty well for himself. One way or another.

I was here because of McJay. It was he who had reminded me that the Major would away all weekend, leaving his flat unoccupied between Friday and Monday. By telling me that, McJay had as good as told me to go and have a look around the place. Though, if challenged, he would be able to deny it.

The fact that McJay had called the Major's London residence a "flat" suggested that he didn't occupy the entire house. As there were only two floors, I guessed that he would either have the entire upper floor or the entire lower one. This wasn't the sort of area where houses would be split into cheap bedsitting rooms.

Apart from an old man walking an old black Labrador, twenty or thirty yards away, the street was deserted, so I casually pushed up the latch on the gate, stepped into the little garden and shut the gate behind me. The essence of housebreaking is to be casual so that if anyone sees you they won't pay you any attention. They will think you are the houseowner or a friend coming to call. Once in the garden, I slipped behind the privet hedge and took my time looking at the house in front of me. It was a blocky house, white and angular like a sugar cube. The door was slap-bang in the middle of the front wall with two windows to its right and two windows to its left. On the second storey, there were five windows, one directly above each of the ground floor windows and another one directly above the door. There was a pale glimmer of light coming from one of the upstairs rooms. Since the Major would, by this time (I hoped!) have left London for his country retreat, I guessed that the upstairs light must belong to the tenant of the other flat. That meant the Major's flat must be on the ground floor, which made the task of breaking and entering a bit simpler. I strolled towards the porch and climbed the three steps to the front door. I was wearing rubber-soled shoes and the path was made of flagstones so I was as quiet as a well-trained alley cat.

There were two bellpushes on the front door and two brass nameplates underneath them. The top floor was occupied by someone called "Miss M. C. Jeevons" and the bottom floor was taken by the Major. The door was fitted with two locks – a big, old-fashioned, easy-to-open one at waist height, and a new, not-so-easy-to-open Yale lock above it. The locks were of no interest to me since I didn't intend breaking in through the front door anyway. Doing so would be sure to attract attention either from a nosy passer-by or from Miss M. C. Jeevons on the top floor.

A small path led around to the back of the house. There wasn't a back garden, just a couple of square yards of flagstones with a rubbish bin and a sickly-looking little tree in an ugly-looking big pot. The back door of the house had an old-fashioned lock but no Yale. The top half of the door had a window made of frosted glass. Shining my torch through the window I could see that the silly bugger had left the key in the keyhole on the inside of the door. Any common thief could have smashed the glass, reached in and turned the key to open the door. I'm not any common thief. I had no intention of smashing the glass. The noise would alert the neighbours, not to mention Miss M. C. Jeevons. I could have cut a hole in the glass with a glass-cutter, of course. But a hole in the window would have given the game away. I didn't want the Major to know that I (or anyone else, come to that) had been inside his place. So I looked around for some other way.

I soon spotted it. There was an old-fashioned sash window to the left of the door – one of those windows made of two sliding frames – a lower frame and an upper frame – with a pulley system so you can slide the lower one up and the upper one down. A burglar's dream! The wood was partly rotten. The easiest way to get inside would have been to give a hefty kick to the frame around the bottom window. It would have been the simplest thing in the world to make the entire frame come loose so I could crawl inside. But, like I said, I didn't want to attract attention and I didn't want to leave any signs of breaking and entering so that was out too.

Besides, there's a better way to get past a sash window – one of those old ones, anyway. Most of them have these dinky little locks that clip the bottom window to the top window. The bottom edge of the top window has a metal catch attached. The top edge of the bottom window has a little lever. To lock the window you just swivel the lever so it goes under the catch. "Lock", did I say? That's a laugh. If you happen to have a nice thin blade with you, which by pure chance I did, and if you also happen to know how to poke that blade through the crack between the two windows and give the little lever just the right sort of flick, which, also by pure chance, I did, then it's a minute's work to open the lock, push up the bottom window and get yourself inside the house without leaving so much as a scratch on the paintwork to show you were ever there. Which is exactly what I did.

Having climbed over the ledge, I gently closed the window and pushed my way through the curtains. They were very nice curtains. Gold velvet on the inside, double-lined to keep in the heat. They also kept in the light which, for a housebreaker, is extremely convenient. I flipped on a small pocket torch and had a good look around the room. It was a bit ornate for my tastes: armchairs and a settee upholstered in cream-coloured satin with gold embroidery; a big mirror in a hideously over-decorated frame, a coffee table, a sideboard, some paintings on the walls. French impressionists, I think. All originals. There was a door on my right. I opened it and walked into a short passageway that ran the length of the house. From there I had a quick shufty in all the other rooms. There was a kitchen, a bathroom, a dining room, a bedroom with a huge double bed, and a small room with a big mahogany desk in the middle and bookshelves all along the walls. I can't describe the rooms in detail, the way an estate agent would, but I can confidently say that I had broken into an elegant and well-appointed apartment in a much sought-after location.

If there was anything of interest to be found, I assumed the best place to look would be in the study. I was wrong about that but bear with me. I'll get around to that shortly. The books were mostly of the sort you buy by the yard – lots of luxury editions in elegant bindings. There was the Complete Works of Dickens, a full set of The Encyclopaedia Britannica, a book on fishing, another on the discovery of the source of the Nile. As far as I could see, none of them had been read. Not recently anyway. But they looked nice.

I opened the drawers in the desk. They contained paper and pens, a pocket French-English dictionary, some loose change, a magnifying glass, a deck of cards, a nail-file and other assorted bits and pieces. There were no secret plans, no bundles of used roubles, no coded instructions to meet Dmitri under the clock in Waterloo Station at 1 o'clock. There was only the kind of stuff you'd expect to find in a desk drawer: paperclips, a few postage stamps, a half-eaten packet of mint imperials.

I had a look at some of the books, just in case there were secret plans and used roubles tucked between their pages. There weren't. So

I carried on hunting around the rest of the flat. To be honest, I didn't have a clear idea what I was looking for. If Major Teddy was up to something that he shouldn't have been up to, he wasn't going to leave incriminating evidence scattered all over his flat. I was just hoping that I'd see something that didn't quite "fit", something that might give me a hint about the sort of man the Major really was.

To be honest, I had qualms about sneaking around the old geezer's digs; not because I have any moral objections to sticking my nose into other people's business. If I had, I'd be in a different job. No, the thing was, the Major was a client. He was employing me to do a job for him. Not so long ago, Meek had suggested breaking into Kitty Brigg's house to look for evidence of her husband's extra-marital activities. I'd informed Meek that in my line of work it's generally considered bad form to break into a client's house and go snooping around in his private affairs. Well, there's a first time for everything.

I poked around the cupboards in the kitchen. There were a few tins of beans, some tea and instant coffee, a packet of cornflakes and some chocolate biscuits. The small fridge contained a bottle of milk, some butter and a bottle of Bollinger Champagne. It looked as though the Major was fussier about what he drank than what he ate. A cupboard to the right of the small electric cooker contained racks of wines, most of them well beyond my price bracket.

Next I looked in the bathroom. This was decorated with lots of marble and a big, ceramic bath. I didn't discover anything suspicious though, unless you count the rubber duck and the large bottle of Monsieur de Givenchy aftershave. I was starting to think the house-breaking was going to lead to another dead end. My luck changed when I went into the bedroom.

It was the double bed that caught my eye. When I'd spoken to her, the Major's wife had told me that she never stayed with her husband in London. Assuming she was telling the truth, the double bed suggested that someone else did. Maybe I'd have got further with this job if, instead of the Major hiring me to look for stolen papers, his wife had hired me to look into his infidelities. It turned out that I'd been going about it all the wrong way. I'd been trying to find someone who'd stolen some trivial-seeming documents on the assumption that the documents themselves were the most important clue. They weren't. The client was the most important clue. From the outset, it had been pretty bloody obvious that Major Willoughby-Styrt hadn't wanted to hire me and was making as little effort as he possibly could to further my investigation. Someone had leaned on him. In all probability someone from McJay's department. Not McJay himself though. He was too far down the food-chain to authorise this kind of investigation. But whoever it was, someone wanted me to follow the investigation wherever it happened to take me. And where it had taken me was into my client's bedroom.

There was a painting of Whitley Bay on the wall. I knew it was Whitley Bay because there was a label on the bottom of the frame that said "Whitley Bay by Moonlight" along with the name of the artist. I don't recall the artist's name. That's no great loss. Anyone who paints Whitley Bay by moonlight deserves to be forgotten. I looked behind the painting, hoping to find a wall safe. All I found was dust.

There was a dinky little bedside cabinet made of white-painted wood with a gold-painted filagree. For all I know it was an invaluable Louis Quinze masterpiece though to my untutored eye it looked like a piece of Petticoat Lane tat. Apart from a half-eaten packed of Fisherman's Friends throat lozenges, the most interesting thing in the cabinet was a paperback Dennis Wheatley novel and a half-empty bottle of Macallan's whisky.

It was when I opened the double doors of the wardrobe, set into a wall alongside the bed, that my luck took a turn for the better. The wardrobe contained rack after rack of suits and shirts, a few pullovers, a couple of overcoats. The suits were of the Savile Row variety. A lot more expensive than their Berwick Street counterparts but unless you bothered to look at the labels you'd never know. I wasn't interested in the labels. I was interested in the pockets. The pockets of a man's jacket sometimes contain dark secrets. The pockets of a man's trousers contain even darker ones. I had a good rummage around to see what I could find. In the jackets I found a variety of coins, an old ticket to a Covent Garden opera, a couple of meal receipts, a half-crushed raspberry ripple and a lot of fluff.

It was when I turned to the trousers that I struck gold. There was a membership card to a private members' club. The card didn't give much away. Printed in plain black lettering was this:

The Basement W1
Private Members' Club

Underneath that someone had written "M273B" followed by an illegible scribble. I guessed M273B might be a code to identify the member without that member having to do anything so indiscreet as to write his name. The squiggle was, I presumed, the authenticating signature of an official of the club. The fact that the details on the card were so limited was the most interesting thing about the card.

The W1 postal district is a big one. It contains most of central London, including the West End and Soho. I had a strong feeling that The Basement would not be the sort of club where elderly gents sat around sipping brandy in leather armchairs. I had a feeling, in fact, that it might be the sort of club of which the Major's wife would not wholeheartedly approve. In fact it might even be the sort of club that offered certain special discreet services of which the Home Office might not wholeheartedly approve. As it turned out, I was right. The club was the answer to everything.

30. A Dangerous Position To Be In

"Drugs."

"What about drugs?"

"That's his business."

"Whose?"

"That Baron bloke. The one who's got a grudge against you."

It was Tuesday morning. A light drizzle was falling. I was bored with life and I had a headache. I was writing up a report for a client on my trusty Imperial 66 typewriter. The client was a man who'd been having a problem with his vegetables. They were prize-winning vegetables: cucumbers, marrows and the like. Someone had been nobbling them – digging them up and pulling off the leaves during the night. I'd watched the garden from the cover of an alleyway. I found the culprit. It was a fox. If you've ever got the impression that a private investigator's life is full of glamour and excitement, I'll be glad to introduce you to the fox.

"Simon Baron?" I said. I was trying to concentrate on the report I was writing. I had to phrase it in such a way that the client ended up thinking he'd got good value for his money. "You think he's selling drugs?"

"I know he is."

"Oh?" I wasn't really listening.

"Not just selling drugs. He does everything from manufacture to distribution."

"Yeah? Oh, bugger!" I'd made a mistake. I'd typed "fux" instead of "fox". Meek has that effect on me. I had to backspace and type three big Xs over the misspelled word. "And how do you know this?"

"That bird, the blonde one."

I pulled the sheet out of the typewriter. The crossed-out word looked unprofessional. I'd have to start all over again. It was only then that I realised what Meek had said. He'd been talking about the blonde girl. I assumed he meant the girl I'd seen Frankie Brigg with. Meek had only gone and followed her, hadn't he!

"You tailed her, then?" I said.

Meek gave a big smile. "I did more than that. I took her out."

"What?"

"Yeah. Down Chelsea way. Went to a restaurant. Wined her and dined her. Prawns. Lobster. Crepes Suzettes. The works."

"You did *what?*"

"Are you deaf or something? I took her for a meal. Just me and her. Candle-lit table. Gypsy violinist playing in the background. Very romantic."

"I thought you said you'd be discreet!"

"A bit rich coming from you, that is. You're the one who went boozing down a pub with Frankie Brigg, the bloke you were being paid to follow. Call that discreet, do you?"

"Yes, well, never mind about that. How did you and this blonde girl get so matey so quickly, then?"

"I followed them. Frankie Brigg and Ophelia…"

"Who?"

"That's her name. Ophelia Monterosa."

"You're kidding me."

Meek gave me a look of withering scorn. "She's one of the Berkshire Monterosas. Daddy's in oil."

"Oil?"

"The black stuff that comes out of the ground."

"I've heard of it."

"He sells it, apparently. By the ship-load."

"Nice business to be in."

"Ophelia thinks it's oppressive. To the proletariat. Which, in case you didn't know, is people like me."

"You were telling me about your candle-lit dinner."

"I had a steak, Ophelia had the fish. We had a couple of bottles of wine and a couple of glasses of brandy to wash it down with."

"How come you're flush with money all of a sudden?" Meek is a notable scrounger who, in my long experience, never has two pennies to rub together.

"I did a small favour for a mate of mine down Wapping and…"

"OK, OK. Never mind the details." I knew enough about Meek's activities to know that I didn't want to know anything about any favours he'd done for his mates down in Wapping. If those favours brought in enough money to splash around on steaks and brandies, there was a very good chance that they were on the wrong side of the law. Whenever possible I like to be ignorant of Meek's dubious dealings. Then, if anyone should ever take me down to the station to have a quiet chat I would be able to say, in all honesty, "Sorry, officer, I don't know anything about it."

I decided I needed to give Meek's story about rich blondes in Chelsea restaurants my undivided concentration so I filled the kettle and plugged it in. The report on the marrow-destroying fox would have to wait.

"Start at the beginning," I said.

"I was watching that building in Kilburn. Just like you told me to."

"I did?"

Meek nodded. "You did. So I went there. Last night."

"And you ended up having a candle-lit dinner with a girl called Ophelia Monterosa?"

Meek nodded again. "That's exactly what happened."

"There's a bit of a gap in this story. How did you go from watching a building to wining and dining a posh blonde bird?"

Meek smirked. "It's easy when you've got the charm."

"So give me the details."

Meek gave me the details in his usual rambling way. What it boiled down to was this. He followed Frankie Brigg from his house, then he followed him on the underground to Kilburn. Frankie Brigg went into Baron's building at 7:30. At eight o'clock he came out again, in the company of the blonde girl. They walked to Kilburn tube station. Frankie Brigg entered the station. The blonde girl didn't. In some mysterious way, which I cannot fathom, Meek then managed to casually "bump into" the girl and strike up a conversation. He offered to take the girl to dinner and the girl accepted.

"This is your standard chat-up technique?" I asked.

Meek shrugged. "I take things as they come."

"So what did you find out?"

"Somewhere between the prawn cocktail and the steak I asked her if she'd heard of RSG-6."

"Very romantic," I said. "Why should she have heard of it?"

"She's one of them ban-the-bombers. A lot of them posh birds are. Anyway, she knew all about this RSG-6 place because a few mates of hers broke into it and nicked some headed notepaper."

"That's probably a hanging offence," I said, meaning it to be a joke. Meek didn't see the joke. He gets very touchy on the subject of legal punishments, be they of the capital, corporal or custodial varieties.

"So then I asked her about Turnstile. She'd never heard of it."

"Shame. I thought you were going to say her daddy owned it."

"Well, he doesn't."

"And did you ask her about Frankie Brigg?"

Meek smirked. "What's it worth?"

"Worth?"

"To you. I've got information that will crack this case wide open. That must be worth a packet."

Crack the case wide open? I thought. It was a bog-standard infidelity job, not Eliot Ness against Al Capone.

"I'll pay for your dinner," I said. "The one you and your blonde lady friend had."

Meek didn't seem impressed. But it was the best deal he was going to get so he told me anyway.

"You heard of LSD?"

Assuming he wasn't talking about pounds, shillings and pence, I guessed he meant lysergic acid diethylamide. I told him so. For a few seconds he was speechless. Then he blurted out, "How did you know that?"

"I read a book once."

"There's a bloke in Pimlico," Meek said. "He makes the stuff."

"LSD?" I said. "Very fashionable, I believe. But hard to get."

"Unless you know the right people," Meek said.

"The blonde girl?"

"Simon Baron."

"Ah. So that's his business?"

"It is. Ophelia isn't involved."

"I'm glad to hear it."

"She just hangs around for the sex."

"Frankie Brigg?"

"Simon Baron. Anyhow, there's this bloke who makes the LSD. Then Baron supplies it to dealers from Land's End to John O'Groats. Ophelia reckons Simon Baron is the second biggest supplier in the country."

"A dangerous position to be in," I said. "I'm guessing the first biggest supplier might not approve of the competition. Still, what Baron gets up to is none of my business."

"Ah, but that's where you are wrong," said Meek. "Because Frankie Brigg is your business. And Frankie Brigg is up to his neck in Simon Baron's business."

Frankie Brigg didn't strike me as the sort of person who'd get intimately involved in the dodgy dealings of a savvy young crook like Simon Baron. The sort of people who got involved with crooks like Simon Baron were grifters and thugs like his two tame henchmen, Mick McManus and Cardew Robinson. Frankie Brigg was a humdrum suburban husband with a humdrum job for a humdrum firm. That was my opinion. I told my opinion to Meek and he agreed with it.

"But there's one thing that's not humdrum about Frankie Brigg," he said. "He's got a secret."

"His nocturnal exploits in the fleshpots of Earls Court? You think that Simon Baron is blackmailing him?"

"Stands to reason, don't it."

"Why would Baron blackmail a suburban accountant? If a crook like Baron wants to blackmail someone, surely he'd blackmail someone rich, otherwise what's the point?"

"The point," said Meek, "is not the money."

"No? Then what is the point?"

"Where does Frankie Brigg work?"

I remembered Meek had told me where he worked, after he'd followed him on the Saturday when I had been otherwise occupied visiting the Major's country residence. But I'd forgotten the details. It hadn't seemed important at the time.

Meek refreshed my memory. "He works for a company called Martin and Whipston. And what do they sell?"

"You tell me."

Meek practically glowed with a self-satisfied air of triumph. "Chemicals is what they sell."

I thought about that for a moment. I remember Meek telling me that he'd seen Frankie Brigg go into his office and come out holding something in a carrier bag. He'd then gone to see Simon Baron and when he'd left he was no longer holding the bag.

"You think he's stealing LSD from a chemicals company?"

"Must be."

"You think a legitimate chemicals company is making LSD, a drug which, as far as I know is not generally available in Boots The Chemist?"

Meek's smug air faded a bit. "Could be."

"Of course it bleeding well couldn't be!" I said. I felt I was getting the better of the argument at last. I'd had enough of being condescended to by Meek. Now it was my turn to give as good as I'd got. "Martin and Whipston probably make fertilisers or liver salts or something. It's a respectable chemicals company, for God's sake, not some seedy little back street operation."

Meek brightened up again when I said that.

"The seedy little backstreet operation is in Pimlico. A bloke called Lozquith. He's from Hungary or Czechoslovakia or one of them places where they all have names full of 'z's and 'q's."

"And how do you even know this bloke called Lozquith exists?"

"Ophelia told me. She said that's where Simon Baron gets the acid."

"I thought he got it from Frankie Brigg."

"Maybe he gets it from both of them? Ophelia was a bit vague. I don't think she gets involved in the business side of things."

"And how did you persuade Ophelia to tell you all this? Was it over the prawn cocktail or the crepe Suzette?"

"It was a bit later on in the evening, as a matter of fact."

31. The Weasel

I didn't feel like going up to town that evening but there was someone I wanted to see. Well, not "wanted" exactly. Nobody in their right minds *wants* to see The Weasel, but sometimes he can be useful. The Weasel lives on the fringes of the London underworld. He knows all the small-time crooks and a few of the big-time ones. If you want to get your hands on cheap booze or some French perfume that fell off the back of a lorry, he'll find ways of supplying them, with discounts for bulk orders. If you want to get hold of blue films or illegal drugs, he'll tell you he doesn't deal in that kind of stuff and then he'll say "but I know someone who does, only it'll cost you extra." I wasn't interested in cheap booze, dodgy French perfume or blue films. But I was interested in drugs.

"What you looking for, Mr Kennick?" he said, his eyes rolling furtively from left to right as though he was expecting the Drug Squad to arrive at any moment. "I can probably lay my hands on some Purples or Blues if that's what you're after. Reefers is no problem. Tell you the honest truth, Mr Kennick, I never knew you partook of that kind of stuff."

We were sitting at a corner table in the Duke Of York pub in Rathbone Street. As long as I've known The Weasel, The Duke Of York has been his regular boozer. Don't ask me why. It's not the worst pub in London but it's not the cocktail bar of The Savoy either. The place stinks of stale beer and the air is thicker than a London smog. As with most central London boozers, it tries to look like a cosy little village pub where everyone knows everyone else but in fact it's bleak and anonymous. Which is maybe why The Weasel likes it so much.

"You heard of LSD?" I said.

The Weasel nearly choked on his double gin. His eyes did the furtive rolling thing again and then he said, in a harsh whisper, "You don't want to be talking so loud, Mr Kennick."

"You know what I'm talking about, then," I said.

He nodded. "Oh, yes. I know all about that. Very trendy it is with teenagers, students, all that lot."

"Do you know who supplies it?"

He'd finished his gin. He stared at the shrivelled lemon slice languishing in the bottom of the glass. I took the glass to the bar and got it topped up with another two measures of gin. I didn't bother getting a new lemon slice. The Weasel wasn't interested in lemons.

"There's a few people who can get it," he said after taking a good slug of gin. "French Pete does a bit, I think. I expect Joe Rawlins could get some. But you probably know about them already."

I had no idea who French Pete or Joe Rawlins were. East End villains, probably. Of no interest to me.

"You heard of a bloke called Simon Baron?"

The Weasel wrinkled his snout. It was his way of showing that he was thinking. Then he took another slug of gin and said, "Name don't ring a bell."

"Maybe you've seen him around then? Young fella. Auburn hair, collar length. Slim, about my height. Bit of a flashy dresser. Seems to work out of Kilburn."

"Oh him!" said The Weasel, his face breaking into a broad smile that revealed his few remaining teeth. "Simon's his name, is it? I never knew that. I just heard him called Baron. Smut is his game. You know, Continental stuff. You seen any of that Continental stuff, Mr Kennick? There's one film with this girl and a horse and…"

I'd already heard more than I wanted to hear about Continental smut. "What I heard was that Baron is in on the LSD lark," I said.

The Weasel shrugged. "Maybe. I never heard about that. The smut is all I heard about. The drugs lark is dangerous, Mr Kennick. He could step on the toes of some of the big boys, if you know what I mean."

"French Pete and Joe Rawlins?" I suggested.

"Bigger than them, Mr Kennick. French Pete and Joe Rawlins is just little cogs in a big machine if you know what I mean. The trouble with young chaps like this Simon Baron is that they want to do everything themselves. They 'as no respect for their elders and betters, if you get my drift."

"Where do people get LSD from anyway?" I asked.

The Weasel gave me a blank look. "How would you expect me to know that, Mr Kennick?"

"I was just hoping, Weasel," I said.

His glass was empty again. He looked at the glass then he looked at me. I ignored him. I didn't plan to spend the rest of the evening nattering to The Weasel. There was information I needed to get about the private life of a certain retired Army Major. The Weasel wasn't the person to give me that information. But I knew who was.

32. The Basement

"Yeah, yeah, I've heard of it. But I didn't think it was your scene, my love."

I was sitting in a pub in Soho trying to figure out why a smart girl like Maggie was eking out a life walking the streets. She had the looks of a film star and a brain as sharp as a knife. She also had a pimp called Eric who wore yellow-checked suits and a greasy trilby hat. I'd asked Maggie once why she didn't get a proper job. She'd given me one of her throaty laughs and said, "I could ask you the same question, my love." She had a point.

Maggie was looking at a small rectangle of crumpled cardboard. It was the membership card that I had purloined from Major Willoughby-Styrt's London residence. The one that said; "The Basement, W1, Private Members' Club".

"What sort of scene is it, exactly?" I asked.

She smiled. "You seem very keen."

"Come on, Maggie. You know me well enough to know that I don't go looking for thrills in seedy basement bars. Apart from anything else, my bank balance couldn't stand the strain. Neither could my heart. These days, I get all my thrills lying alone in my flat with a mug of Horlicks and an Ed McBain novel."

She raised an elegant eyebrow and puckered her lips. "I couldn't care less what you do for fun. Your vices are your own business."

"So what kind of club is it?"

"You don't know?"

"I don't know."

"It's a queer club."

For a second I was lost for words. The Major was a married man. A middle-aged married man with an impeccable reputation and a tailor in Savile Row. Why would he be going to a queer club? A moment's thought on that subject suggested an answer so obvious that I won't even bother telling you what it was.

"So which bit of Soho is this club in, exactly?"

"Not much of a detective are you! You've got all the questions. I've got all the answers."

"That's what detecting is," I said. "Asking all the right questions to people who know all the right answers. I knew you wouldn't let me down, Maggie. Another drink?"

She passed her empty glass to me. The juniper smell made me feel queasy. I went to the bar, being careful not to knock myself senseless on the fake Tudor beams arranged dangerously at head height. I bought a double gin for Maggie and a half of bitter for me.

"You're still looking for the killer, then?" Maggie said as she slugged back the gin.

I didn't at first know what she was talking about. My confusion must have shown. "The last time I saw you," she said, "you were looking for whoever it was who'd bumped off Nate Welbridge."

A piece suddenly slotted itself into my mental jigsaw. On that occasion I'd been trying to find The Blue Canary, the porno shop that McJay had told me about. It had been Maggie who'd told me how to find it. It had also been Maggie who'd told me that Nathen Welbridge hadn't been interested in girls. "Corporal" Nathan Welbridge, the man who'd been killed during the Civil Defence exercise in Bully Fen, had been a homosexual. And now Maggie was telling me that the membership card I'd found in the Major's trouser pocket was for a homosexual nightclub. I didn't immediately see the connection but I was sure there must be one.

Blackmail?

I thought of Frankie Brigg. Then I thought of Simon Baron. Frankie was, I suspected, being blackmailed by Baron. He was being blackmailed to break the law. To obtain drugs for illicit purposes. Was it likely that the Major was being blackmailed too? Not for drugs but for something more dangerous? Secrets.

"Are you sure it's a queer club?" I said.

She smiled and downed the rest of the gin in her glass. "Let's just say that if I tried touting for business there, I'd end up starving."

I bought Maggie another gin. She told me where to find The Basement Club. Then I left.

It wasn't in Soho. It was located somewhere in that warren of streets just south of Marylebone. It didn't take me long to find. It looked like a big but fairly ordinary house in a small but fairly ordinary street. The house has three storeys and a basement. There was a small set of steps that led down from street level to the basement. There was no indication that a club existed there. It gave the impression of being an ordinary basement in an ordinary house in an ordinary street. Its camouflage was perfect.

33. A Two-Mug Problem

The more I knew about the bomb job, the less sense it made. The infidelity job had run into a dead end. I didn't have any other jobs on the go. So on Friday morning I had a bit of a lie in. It was half past ten by the time I strolled along to the office. Meek was already there, with his feet up on my desk and the cat asleep in his lap.

"You're bright and early," I said.

"The sun's shining, the birds are twittering. I thought you'd be glad to see me. I made the tea."

I felt the tea pot. It was hot so I poured myself a mug. I smelled the half-empty bottle of milk standing in the sink. It was only slightly sour so I poured some into my tea, then sat in the chair next to Meek's chair, put my feet up on the desk next to Meek's feet and said, "You're in a good mood this morning. What happened? Did you back the winner at Goodwood?"

"I'm in a good mood because I've got good news."

I sipped my tea, trying to ignore all the little white blobs of sour milk floating around on its scummy surface. "Put me out of my misery. What's the good news?"

"Developments. On the infidelity job."

"Oh, yeah?" Since I didn't know of any developments on that job and since Meek wasn't helping me with my investigations, I didn't allow myself to get over excited. I was expecting him to come up with one of his long, rambling and totally incorrect "theories". Meek's idea of detection is mostly based on crime films. He thinks cases are solved by sudden flashes of inspiration rather than grinding hard work. "Go on, then," I said. "Tell me."

"Frankie Brigg. Half past six last night, he leaves his house…"

"You'd know this, would you?"

"I would."

I put my mug of tea on the desk, sat up straight in my chair and stared at Meek. "You're saying you followed him?"

"That's what I'm saying."

"I never told you to follow him."

"I was acting on my initiative."

This was news to me. Meek and initiative don't, as a rule, go together.

"So, you watched his house, on your own initiative, and at half past six he left?"

"He did."

"And you followed him?"

"I did. Guess where he went."

The day before had been Thursday. One of Frankie's regular nights out. So I reckoned I could make a pretty good guess. "Kilburn," I said.

"Nope."

I made another guess. "Earls Court."

"Bayswater."

"He went to Bayswater? What the hell's in Bayswater?"

"A meeting. About twenty people there, I'd say. In the upstairs room of a pub."

I drank my tea. Said nothing. Watched the fly buzzing around the room. Glanced at the horrible little shepherdess statuette which was still plonked centre-stage on my desk. I'd have to have words with Meek about that. It was starting to depress me.

"So," I said, "are you, or are you not, going to tell me? Frankie Brigg went to a meeting. What sort of meeting?"

"Ban-the-bomb."

I put my tea down. The fly sounded louder in the silence. "You're kidding me."

"Why would I do that? He goes to a room up above a pub. I follow him. He goes in. I go in. He sits down. I sit down."

"And then what?"

"They talk. Some geezer calls the room to order. Reads the minutes of the last meeting. Says that books and pamphlets are available for a small fee."

"You bought some?"

"Give over! How thick do you think I am?"

I glanced at the statuette. An answer to Meek's question flitted through my mind but I didn't think Meek would appreciate it.

"Anyway, I had to sit in this poky little room on a hard wooden chair for the best part of an hour listening to these miserable gits whining on about politics, nuclear bombs, the downtrodden proletariat, how to bring about world peace, all that kind of bollocks."

"Didn't they think that was a bit funny? You sitting in their meeting, I mean?"

"I said I was thinking of joining them."

"Give over!"

"Why not?"

"You're one of the least peaceful people I know."

"They don't know that, though, do they?"

"I hate to be the person to break this to you, Meek, but you look like a thug. You're six foot-two, you've got muscles on your muscles and you've got the sort of face that makes old ladies run across the road to avoid you. Whereas your average peacenik is small, pale, thin and steps over the cracks in the pavements to avoid treading on the dandelions."

"Yeah, well that's where you are wrong. This ban-the-bomb mob has all sorts going there. Not just beatniks and Communists. There was a brickie from Clapham and some old girl who writes cookery books. There was even a vicar!"

I finished my tea, stood up, walked to the front window and peered through the venetian blinds. An old man, a tramp, was shuffling past, muttering to himself. I wondered how he'd ended up like that – unwashed, dressed in a filthy overcoat, roaming around on the streets. He can't have been born to that life. There must have been a time before. Maybe he'd had a good job but then he took to the bottle? Maybe he'd had a wife and kids but they'd come to a sticky end and the tragedy had unhinged him? Maybe he…

"…found out exactly what Frankie Brigg gets up to." I hadn't been paying attention to what Meek was saying. "Frankie Brigg," he repeated. "I know where he goes, what he does and who he does it with."

I turned away from the venetian blinds and stared at Meek.

"You haven't been listening to me, have you?" he said.

"'Course I have." I sat down in my chair and gave Meek my full attention. "So he went to a ban-the-bomb meeting. And after that was over, what happened? He went somewhere else?"

"He went to a pub."

"I thought you said he was already in a pub, that the meeting was in the upstairs room of a pub."

"It was. In Bayswater. He went to another pub."

"In Bayswater?"

"In Earls Court. Him and some other bloke, who was also in the ban-the-bomb meeting."

"You followed him?"

"'Course I bleedin' followed him!"

"And *did* he…?"

"Did he what?"

"I don't know. I mean, when he got to this pub, in Earls Court did he meet a voluptuous widow? Did this voluptuous widow take him back to her charming little end-of-terrace house? Once they were in the house did she throw him onto the deep-pile shag carpet of her sumptuous living room and make wild passionate love to him?"

Meek was giving me one of his blank-eyed stares. "What are you on about? End-of-terrace house? Shag carpet? What's that got to do with anything?"

Meek has a very literal mind. I, on the other hand, have a tendency to let my imagination run away with me. This often leads to awkward misunderstandings. "Never mind the details," I said. "Has he got a mistress? And, if so, who is she?"

"I couldn't say for sure…" he said, "but I very much doubt it. How well do you know Earls Court?"

"Not very well."

"Do you know a pub called the Lord Ranelagh?"

"No."

"Well, that's where Frankie Brigg and his friend went. I didn't follow."

"Why not?"

"The Lord Ranelagh is a queer pub."

"There's a lot of it about," I said, thinking about the secretive Basement club.

"So anyway, I don't think Frankie has a fancy woman after all. I reckon he's got a fancy man."

That, I thought, was a complication I could well do without. Kitty Brigg owed me money. In order to get that money, I'd have to tell her that her husband was having it away with a bloke. I wasn't sure she'd consider me to be the bearer of glad tidings. Some people are funny that way. If you give them good news, they give you a bonus. Give them bad news and they don't want to give you anything.

"Oh, and there's another thing," Meek added.

"What other thing would that be?"

"I saw Ophelia again."

"The blonde girl."

"The very one."

"And…?"

"That Simon Baron bloke."

"What about him?"

"Seems you've rubbed him up the wrong way."

"With my sunny personality? I can't think why."

"Yeah, well, Ophelia reckons Baron might have plans. To deal with you, if you get my drift."

"Go on," I said, "tell me all about it."

I could tell this was going to be a two-mug problem, so I filled up the kettle, put some fresh tea into the pot and rearranged the cat on my lap.

34. Breaking News

Over the weekend, I tried to think of a gentle way of breaking the bad news to Kitty Brigg. I couldn't think of one. Infidelity cases are always awkward. I've done lots of jobs where the husband was two-timing his wife with a woman. But I'd never had a job before where the husband was two-timing his wife with a man. I hesitated before picking up the phone. I wasn't sure how Mrs Brigg would take the news.

"Don't let me stop you."

The bell on the door tinkled as Meek came in, followed closely by the cat. I put the phone down. "I was just about to make some tea."

Meek went to the window ledge, picked up the bottle of milk, gave it a quick sniff and said, "I think I'll pass on the tea. This stuff's turned into yoghurt. Like I was saying, don't let me stop you phoning whoever it was you was about to phone."

"Oh, it wasn't urgent," I said. "It'll wait."

Meek poured some milk into a saucer and put it on the floor. Straker gave it a sniff and decided he was having nothing to do with it. Then Meek sat in a chair and Straker sat on Meek.

"Tell you the truth," I said, "I was about to phone Mrs Brigg."

Meek smiled broadly. "That'll be interesting. Don't mind me. You phone her. I promise I won't laugh."

"Your compassion knows no bounds," I said. Then I had an idea. "It should be you who phones her, not me."

"Me! I don't think so."

"You keep saying you want to learn the business. That's part of the business. Besides which, it was you who followed Frankie Brigg. Which means it was your investigation. If she's got any questions, it's you who'll have the answers."

"OK," he said. "I can't see what all the fuss is about. It's only a phone call, after all. I pick up the phone. I tell her that her husband's been doing dirty deeds with some geezer in Earls Court and, by the way, we'd appreciate prompt payment of our bill. A doddle. Hand me the phone."

I slid the phone across the desk.

"I'm going down the newsagents' to get a paper," I said. "Do it while I'm gone."

Meek was picking up the phone as I went through the door. The bell tinkled behind me. It was a sunny morning, little fluffy clouds drifted across a pale blue sky, the air was scented with the delicate perfume of exhaust fumes. It was a great day to be alive. And, at that very moment, I thought to myself, a young woman's life was about to be torn apart. There was no easy way to break news of that sort but it was I who should be doing the breaking, not an insensitive lout like Meek.

I turned around, swung open the door and strode back into the office. Meek was talking into the phone. I snatched the receiver from his hand and said, "Hello, this is Kennick. I don't know what my assistant's been saying to you but I think we need to talk about this calmly…"

There was silence at the other end of the line. Then there was a voice. A man's voice. It said, "So do you want me to do it or don't you?"

"Sorry?" I said. "Who is this?"

"Who'd you bloody well think it is?" The man's voice was becoming more annoyed-sounding. "It's Alf Beedle, who else would it be?"

Meek, I saw, had his elbows on his desk with his chin resting on his fists. He was smirking.

"Alf Beedle?" I said.

"The bookmaker in Bridge Street. Mr Meek wanted me to place a bet on Florry's Delight in the 2.30 at…"

I handed the receiver back to Meek. He had never had any intention of phoning Mrs Brigg. I'd been taken for a chump. Maybe that's what I am, when it comes down to it – a chump.

35. The Butterfly Business

I drank two mugs of tea and then I made a phone call. Meek had sloped off by that time and there was just me and Straker manning the office. My phone call was to a man called Billie Armless. He real name is Billie Silver. They call him Billie Armless because his left arm hasn't worked properly ever since he blew up a garage in Clapham. He had been working in the garage at the time of the explosion. Doing chemistry. Billie makes drugs. The sort that get bought and sold on the streets and in some of the swishier nightclubs. I've known Billie for years. He's a bright, funny chap, in his late thirties, fair hair, sharp suits, talks with a plummy accent. Not your usual lowlife villain. It's rumoured he studied chemistry at one of the older universities – Oxford or Cambridge – but was sent down for spiking the fellows' drinks with mescaline. I doubt if the story is true, though Billie has never denied it.

"Kennick!" he said. "So lovely to hear from you after all this time. Are you still in the debt-collecting business?"

He knew I was a private detective but he pretended to think I was a debt collector. He did it to irritate me. I didn't correct him. I wouldn't give him the satisfaction.

"Billie," I said, "I need a favour."

"If it is within my capacities to provide such a favour, naturally I shall do my utmost."

Billie has a way of talking that's like a bank manager who's about to break the bad news that your account's in arrears and if you don't pay it off by the end of the week he'll be sending the boys around to sort you out.

"What do you know about LSD?" I said.

"Fuck me!" Billie replied. He wasn't sounding quite so bank-managerish now.

"Thanks for the offer," I said. "But I'd rather you just told me what you know about LSD."

"You want some?"

"Not personally."

"You know it's illegal."

"So I assumed."

"Only just, though."

"What d'you mean, 'only just'? It's either legal or it's illegal. That's how the law works."

"The thing is, it used to be legal. Maybe it still is. Then again, I'm not entirely certain. You see, LSD was thought to be harmless, unlike amphetamines, say. People take it, giggle a lot and decide that butterflies hold the secrets of the universe. But then the Home Secretary, being something of a grouchy old soul, decided that giggling and butterflies were bad for morale and had a tendency to deprave and corrupt. He kicked up a bit of a fuss with the result that the House Of Lords brought in an amendment to the Drugs (Prevention of Misuse) Act of 1964 to make possession of LSD illegal."

"So it is illegal?"

"Not yet. I believe we are free to indulge for a few more weeks. If you want to giggle at butterflies, now would be the perfect time. But the law is on the cusp of a change and soon if we are found in the company of butterflies we shall be banged up in Reading Jail or wherever it is they put the reprobates these days."

"So LSD is legal now. But in in a few weeks it won't be?"

"Precisely."

I mulled that over. Simon Baron was trading in LSD. So he could claim to be a legitimate businessman for the time being. But in a few weeks he would be a criminal.

"Do you make the stuff?" I asked.

He laughed. "I wouldn't tell you if I did. But since I don't, I will tell you. No. There are very few people who do. The ingredients are somewhat difficult to obtain."

"The ingredients being…?"

"I couldn't give you the full recipe, but ergotoxine would be the crucial starting point."

"And ergotoxine is what?"

"It's a drug. Derived from a fungus, I believe."

"And apart from making LSD, what else is it used for?"

"To the best of my knowledge, it is used by the medical profession to treat thyroid problems."

"Where would someone go to buy ergotoxine ?"

"I think Germany is the main source. You'd either have to smuggle it in or else you could probably get it from one of the commercial chemical importers."

So that's what Frankie was making silently disappear from the stock-book of Martin and Whipston Chemicals!

"What will happen to the black market trade in LSD when it becomes illegal?" I asked.

"Business will boom, naturally. As far as the supply network is concerned, prohibition is the best thing that could happen."

36. A Job Well Done

I couldn't put it off any longer. On Tuesday morning, I got into the office just after ten. I put a couple of sardines in a saucer for Straker and I put the kettle on to boil. I sat behind my desk and picked up the phone. She answered on the second ring.

"Ah, Mrs Brigg," I said. "It's Mr Kennick."

I was waiting for her to say something. After a few seconds, she did. "Mr Kennick," she said. "Nothing wrong, is there?"

I loosened my tie. Straker leapt onto my lap. I clenched my teeth and tried not to groan. "The investigation. There have been developments."

"Really? I don't follow."

"Your husband. We were able to locate him. Last Thursday. I would have phoned earlier, but, naturally, I had to verify certain, well, details and…"

I told her about her husband's visit to the Lord Ranelagh pub. Her reaction wasn't what I'd been expecting.

"Oh, that pub in Earls Court. I know all about that. Your assistant gave me the details."

"My assistant?"

"Gordon."

"Gordon?" For a moment, I couldn't think who she was talking about.

"Gordon Meek," she said. "Your assistant."

"Oh, *that* Gordon!"

I tried to make sense of what she was telling me. The previous day, when I'd told Meek to phone Mrs Brigg, he'd called his bookmaker.

"You understand what sort of men go to the Lord Ranelagh pub?" I said.

"Gordon explained everything. It's where the fairies go."

"Your husband was…"

"He was having a bit of slap and tickle with a fella. You don't have to mince words with me, Mr Kennick. I haven't lived a sheltered life, you know."

"And that doesn't bother you?"

"I should say it doesn't! A blessed relief is what it is. If he'd been having it away with another woman, that would have been a different kettle of fish. But a man, that's not what you'd call competition, is it?"

"Isn't it?"

I still wasn't sure that she fully understood the nature of her husband's indiscretions. So I filled in a few of the details, including his friend, Pete, the chap I'd met in the pub on the occasion when he and Frankie Brigg had given me the slip and gone off to Earls Court together. I gave her a description of Pete: tall fair, curly hair, double-breasted suit, said he was an accountant.

Kitty Brigg laughed: "Accountant! That's a good one! His name's Trevor, not Pete. He works for one of the department stores on Regent's Street. I've always thought he was a bit 'that way'. He wears too much aftershave, if you know what I mean. I wonder why he gave you a false name? Maybe he could tell you were a detective?"

I am rarely at a loss for words. I've done plenty of infidelity jobs. I once had to break the news to a respectable middle-aged woman from Ruislip that her respectable, middle-aged husband was having an affair with a seventeen year-old Algerian stripper. On another occasion, I found out that a thirty-five year old suburban bank manager was visiting a bordello in Brighton once a month when he'd told his wife he was going on training courses. The wives' reactions varied between hysteria (the bank manager's wife) to quiet resignation (the woman from Ruislip). I'd never had a reaction like Kitty Brigg's before and, to be frank, I didn't know how to deal with it.

Still, if Kitty Brigg was happy then that was that. All I was interested in was collecting the outstanding payment. I mentioned that. She said, "Oh, but I paid your assistant."

"Gordon?" I asked.

"Mr Meek," she confirmed.

The kettle was whistling so I wished Mrs Brigg a good day, put down the phone and went to make the tea. Half an hour later, Meek staggered in, looking very much the worse for wear. There were a few things I needed to discuss with him.

"I was talking to a friend of yours on the phone," I said.

Meek scooped up the cat and slumped down into the chair he'd been occupying. "Oh yeah? Who would that be?"

"A client of mine."

"Ah." I got the feeling he knew which client.

"She gave you a cheque, I am led to believe."

Meek rummaged around inside the pocket of his jacket and eventually produced a crumpled piece of paper that bore a passing resemblance to a cheque. "Don't look at me like that," he said. "It's not as though I was planning to spend it."

"No?"

"No. It's got your name on it."

I glanced at the cheque. It was made out to "Kennick Investigations".

"I'm surprised you didn't tell her to make it out to you."

"I never thought of that." He smiled weakly. "I'm joking." He groaned. The cat had just jumped onto his lap.

"So, tell me all," I said. "How was it that you had a meeting with a client of mine? Without even telling me."

"It just sort of happened."

"*What* just sort of happened?"

"I happened to be walking down Willow Street last night…"

"Where Mr and Mrs Brigg live."

"Except Mr Brigg – Frankie, that is – goes out on Monday and Thursday evenings…"

"I am aware of that."

"And yesterday evening, being a Monday…"

"He was out."

"So I called in."

I glared at Meek. "You just happened to call in?"

"That's right."

"To see Mrs Brigg?"

"That's right. Kitty, as I call her. So I…"

I put my head in my hands. "Don't tell me. Oh, God, Meek, please don't tell me that you seduced a client."

"Me? What? Nah."

"Thank God for that!"

"Well, what I mean to say is, she's not a client of *mine*, is she? And, anyway, I wouldn't say I seduced her. I offered her some comfort. In her time of need. What with her husband being out cavorting with a bunch of shirt-lifters."

I groaned. And this time the cat wasn't to blame.

37. Business In Pimlico

Wednesday morning, Meek was in a good mood and so was the cat. I could tell he was in a good mood because he kept rubbing himself up against my legs. The cat, I mean. I could tell Meek was in a good mood because he told me he was.

"I'm in a good mood," he said.

The cat is usually in a good mood when he's had a good night hunting. That morning he was looking fatter than the night before and he didn't miaow for his breakfast. He just jumped up onto his chair, settled down on the cushion and fell fast asleep.

"Caught a rat," I said.

Meek smiled. "You could say that."

"I was talking about the cat."

"That makes two of us, then."

It was too early in the morning for sparkling repartee. It was barely ten o'clock. Meek's rarely awake at that ungodly hour. Unless he's made a night of it and hasn't bothered going to bed. But I could tell from his bright-eyed, fresh-faced look that he had not come into the office directly after a night of boozing and debauchery. So I put on the kettle, scooped the cat off the cushion, sat down, scooped the cat into my lap, and prepared myself to listen to whatever it was that Meek was so eager to tell me.

"I had an interesting evening yesterday," Meek said.

"Oh yes?"

"I went to Pimlico."

"Very nice at this time of year, I'm told."

"Well?"

"Well what?"

"Ain't you gonna ask me what I was doing in Pimlico?"

As a rule I don't go out of my way to find out what Meek does with in his spare time. I'm not interested in his sex life and I try to know as little as possible about his other activities.

"Since you haven't asked," he said, "I'll tell you."

The kettle was whistling. It's a modern kettle – one of those chromium affairs that plugs into a wall-socket but with a good old-fashioned whistle on its spout. At that moment, the whistle provided a useful interruption. I am not what is popularly known as a "morning person". That's one reason I like my job. I work late and I get up late. I like to spend my mornings drinking tea and doing a leisurely crossword. Listening to Meek is not one of my favourite morning activities. I brewed the tea, handed him a mug of it, put my mug onto the desk and rearranged the cat on my lap.

"So," I said, "tell away. What were you doing in Pimlico?"

"I went because of Ophelia."

"Ophelia?"

"You know. The blonde girl. The one who hangs out with that Simon Baron fella."

"I know who she is. What I don't know is the Pimlico connection."

"I told you before. I took her for a candle-lit dinner. She told me about a bloke in Pimlico. You said you'd pay for the dinner."

"I said that?"

Meek gave me one of his withering looks. Withering looks have no effect on me so he stopped withering at me and carried on with his story. "You remember the bloke I mentioned?"

"No."

"The bloke in Pimlico."

"Remind me."

"A fella called Lozquith. Foreigner. He has a nice little business making LSD."

"Oh, *that* bloke in Pimlico!"

"As it happened, yesterday evening I had a bit of time on my hands so I went to have a look at his gaff. I knocked on his door."

"Subtle," I said.

"And this little middle-aged, balding bloke answered it. 'Mr Lozquith?' I said. 'Who wants to know?' says he. 'I'm doing a survey for the Council,' I say. 'You might be entitled to a grant.' So he wants to know what sort of grant and I tell him it's a grant to help small businesses. 'By the way,' says I, 'what sort of business do you run here?'"

"And he, no doubt, tells you he makes drugs," I said satirically.

Meek's not good at satire. "No, that's not what he said."

"Tell me then. What did he say?"

"He shut the door in my face."

"And that's why you are in a good mood? That's what you consider to be a successful day's investigating?"

Once again, my satirical tone was lost on Meek.

"I had a rolled-up newspaper in my hand."

"Is that significant?"

"When he shut the door, I shoved the rolled-up newspaper in the gap. The result being that the door didn't shut."

"Let me guess. You gained entry to his establishment without being invited."

"We had a nice, cosy little chat."

"I can imagine."

"Well. Do you want to know or don't you?"

"I want to know."

So Meek told me.

38. Two Jobs, One Motive?

I was on edge all evening. I tried lying on my sofa and reading a book. I couldn't concentrate. I turned on the TV. Then I turned it off again. I was in no mood for The Wednesday Play. I was in no mood for anything. That was the problem. My mind was focussed on one thing and one thing only. The bomb job. I had all the information now, I was sure of it. I just couldn't quite piece it together to make sense of it all.

This is what I knew. On Friday the 22nd of July I get a phone call from Major Edward Willoughby-Styrt who arranges a meeting for the Sunday at a Civil Defence exercise in Bully Fen, Hackney. He tells me that some top-secret documents have been stolen but, apart from a trivial inventory of pencils and toilet rolls he doesn't tell me what they are.

After a bit of investigating, it seems to me that the obvious suspect is a not-very-lovable bloke called Frank Featherglade: he had been in the underground bunker alone with the Major's attaché case on the weekend when the documents had disappeared; moreover, he worked in the Major's office, so probably had a pretty good idea about the sort of documents the Major kept in his attaché case. Everything pointed to Featherglade being the thief. Only I didn't think he was. It was all too neat, too obvious.

I couldn't shake the feeling that Featherglade was the fall-guy. Somebody has set him up. In which case, who was that somebody? The only realistic possibility was Major Edward Willoughby-Styrt. I only had his word that the attaché case had been with him throughout that weekend except for a few moments when Featherglade had been left alone with it in an underground bunker.

If Featherglade was innocent, then who was guilty? The Major was the most obvious suspect. For all I knew, he might have been passing secret information to the Soviets for years. But this time he had had the misfortune to be found out when his assistant, Gregory

O'Donnell, looked for some documents on the Monday morning and had found that they had gone AWOL over the weekend.

What was the Major's motive? Money? Sympathy for the Communist cause? Fear? The Major stole secrets. Frankie Brigg stole drugs. Two very different people with one thing in common – fear of exposure. Baron, I reckoned, had been blackmailing Frankie Brigg. Someone, I guessed, had been blackmailing the Major. If only I could find out who it was, maybe everything else would fall into place?

Meek had extracted the details of Frankie Brigg's involvement in Simon Baron's seedy business from Andris Lozquith, the man he'd visited in Pimlico. Meek and Lozquith had had a nice, friendly chat and Lozquith had been only too happy to tell Meek everything he wanted to know. Meek's nice friendly chats tend to have that effect on people.

To be honest, I'd already figured out most of it but, even so, it was nice to have confirmation. Lozquith makes the drug, Baron distributes it. Lozquith puts drops of LSD onto tiny bits of blotting paper. One bit of blotting paper is enough for one "trip". I was starting to wonder if that was where Baron's supposed trade in knick-knacks might come into the picture. Maybe he was sending boxes of cheap china ornaments the length and breadth of the country while, hidden deep inside their cheap china bodies were the real goods? The LSD.

But, as Billie Armless had explained to me, in order to make LSD you need to start with another chemical called ergotoxine. That's where Frankie Brigg came into the picture. He ordered the drug from his company's suppliers in Germany then, with a few deft changes to the stock books, he made some of it disappear. It disappeared in the general direction of Simon Baron. I wasn't interested in Baron's business. I never had been. He was a minor detail in a different investigation – the infidelities of Frankie Brigg. Now that the infidelity job was over and done with, I hoped I'd never see Baron again. But life isn't always that simple.

*

I went to the pub. Meek was there. I told him everything I'd worked out to see if he could find any flaws in my reasoning. Meek may not be the quickest thinker I've ever met but he understands how the criminal mind works. He had a think about, then he nodded. "Sounds reasonable," he said. Which, by Meek's standards, is high praise.

"There's just one thing that's bothering me," I said.

"Oh yeah?" said Meek. "What's that?"

"The bloke who was killed. Welbridge. Down in Bully Fen."

Meek drank up his beer and wiped the foam off his top lip. "Yeah. What about him?"

"Well, if he's somehow connected with the Major, what's the connection?"

"That's obvious, ain't it?" said Meek, handing his empty glass to me.

"OK," I said. "Put me out of my misery."

"You reckon someone's been blackmailing the Major, yeah?"

"It seems a reasonable hypothesis."

"It was Welbridge. He was the blackmailer."

I froze with Meek's empty glass in my hand. It sounded plausible. According to Maggie, Nathan Welbridge had been a homosexual. Maybe he'd met the Major at The Basement Club or some other secretive establishment. Maybe they'd met in the toilets of Piccadilly tube station or in the bushes of Hampstead Heath. The details were unimportant. What was important was the fact that Welbridge knew who the Major was. He must have seen him, and recognised him, at one of the Civil Defence exercises. With that knowledge, he was in the perfect position to blackmail him. That much made sense. But there was a problem. "I was with the Major at the time Welbridge was killed."

"Oh deary me, you are a bit thick, ain't you!" guffawed Meek. "The Major wouldn't do his own messy work, would he? He'd get someone else to do it. Which not only means he keeps his hands clean but, since you were with him at the time, it also gives him a cast-iron alibi."

I bought a pint for Meek and added on a whisky chaser. As an afterthought, I bought a packet of cheese and onion crisps. I had a feeling Meek had just slotted the last piece into the jigsaw. Well, the last-but-one piece. If the Major had arranged for Welbridge to be bumped off, he had an accomplice, someone who'd stuck the knife between Welbridge's fourth and fifth ribs. I needed to find out who that was.

39. Rat Trap

I had a good, long sleep that night. By the time I got into my office the following morning, I knew there was only one way to find out who the killer was. I would have to talk to the person who had hired him. I picked up the phone. I dialled a number that McJay had given me. A brisk woman's voice answered. I told her to put me through to Major Willoughby-Styrt. "May I ask if the Major is expecting your call, sir?" She sounded like she'd been sucking lemons. "Yes, you may ask," I replied, "and I may decline to answer." She made a choking noise. Maybe a lemon pip had gone down the wrong way. She could, she explained, not put "just anyone" through to the Major and, besides, she would really rather like to know how I had obtained this telephone number. I informed her that I was not "just anyone", I was, in fact, the one person in all the world to whom Major Willoughby-Styrt needed to speak at his earliest opportunity, what's more it was none of her damned business how I'd obtained this phone number and if she didn't put me through pretty damn' quick, the next phone call she'd be getting would come straight from the Home Secretary.

I was, of course, bluffing. The Home Secretary didn't know me and if he had known me he would probably have crossed the street to avoid me. But I'm a good bluffer. So good, in fact, that at that moment I almost believed my own bluff. Anyway, five seconds later, Major Willoughby-Styrt was on the line.

"We have to meet," I said.

"Why? Have you found out… well, you know?"

"We have to meet," I repeated. I wasn't giving anything away until I saw him face to face. I had a feeling he wouldn't like what I'd found out. And if he didn't like it, he might make things awkward for me. Anyway, after a bit of blustering we eventually agreed that I would come to his house that evening. He gave me the address. I pretended not to know where it was. I didn't mention that I'd already been there. That's another thing he might not have liked.

*

The house looked different by daylight. It was just as square, just as Victorian, the columns around the porch were just as Roman and the privet hedge growing behind the garden wall was just as privetty as they had been on the evening when I'd broken in. But by daylight, it looked more impressive. I'm not sure why. Maybe it was the stark whiteness of its walls contrasting with the ebony black of its front door. Or maybe it was due to the fact that I'd walked all the way up the street and had, as a consequence, had a good look at all the other houses with their stark white facades and their pseudo Greek and Roman columns and I knew that the people who lived in these houses were not the sort of people who mixed with people like me. They were the ruling classes. I was one of the people they ruled.

I pressed the front door bell. It made a decorous ding-dong sound somewhere deep inside the house. I waited. No answer. I waited a bit more. Still no answer. I was about to press the bell again when I heard the sound of footsteps making their way slowly up the hallway towards the door. The Major was not the sort of person who would open the door in a hurry to tradesmen, hawkers, private investigators or other riff-raff.

The door opened. "Mr Kennick."

"May I come in?"

The bastard would have kept me standing on the step if it had been up to him.

He gave me a snake-like smile. "Of course, of course. Please, dear fellow, *do* come in!"

He was overdoing the bonhomie. It was aimed at making me feel uneasy. It didn't work. He led the way down the passage towards the back of the house. The wallpaper, I noted, was green-and-red striped. The last time I'd been there I'd only had the light of my torch to see by so I hadn't had the opportunity to take in the full garishness of the bilious colour-scheme.

"Please, come into the lounge."

He opened the door. We went into the room I'd broken into. I wondered whether I should tell him about the poor security of his sash windows.

"Take a seat, Mr Kennick."

He gestured towards the cream-coloured settee trimmed with gold embroidery and tassels. It was even more hideous by the light of day than it had been by the light of my torch.

"You seemed most eager to speak to me, Mr Kennick. Might I ask what occasioned your zeal?"

"I've discovered something that, well, not to put too fine a point on it…"

This was the first time I'd had to tell a client that I suspected that he had been selling top secret documents to enemies of our country because he was being blackmailed and that, furthermore, I had good reason to believe he may be an accessory to a murder.

"Not to put too fine a point on *what*, Mr Kennick?" The Major sat in a big armchair, crossed one leg over the other and took a cigarette from a gold case that was lying open on an occasional table. "Care for a cigarette, old man?"

I declined the offer.

"A whisky, then? I have quite a decent Macallan." He lit his cigarette, inhaled languidly and then let out a long, slow stream of smoke.

The door to the room opened and a man walked in. He was holding a bottle of Macallan in one hand and a stack of three crystal tumblers in the other hand.

My jaw dropped.

I felt like a rat that's walked into a trap.

"How lovely to see you again, Kennick." The voice had that perfectly modulated, oily quality that indicates good-breeding, a public school education and a deep contempt for the human race.

"Becker!" I said. "What the fuck's going on?"

I've known Becker for years. Ever since our Army days. He was an officer. I wasn't. Some officers have the ability to command respect. Other officers are like Becker. When I left the Army I assumed it would be the last I'd ever see of him. No such luck. Becker had been recruited to a furtive branch of the security services which occasionally has to undertake jobs that the less furtive branches won't even admit to. That's where I come in. They need people who can do jobs quickly, efficiently and without too many moral scruples. There are not many of us around.

Usually it's beneath his dignity to deal directly with low-level scum like me. As a rule, he passes his commands onto other chaps of his own class – people whose good-breeding is better than mine but not as good as Becker's. People like Turlough McJay. For Becker to come to see me in person was an unusual honour. It meant things were even more fucked up than I'd assumed they were.

"I do apologise," he said, "for all the rigmarole."

Becker sat in an armchair next to the Major and poured a few fingers of whisky into each of the three crystal tumblers that he'd been holding. He handed one of the glasses to me. I took a swift gulp. I needed it.

"You've done good work on this, Kennick," Becker said. As a rule, he wasn't free with his compliments so I raised my glass in silence and tried not to choke on the whisky.

"Though," he added, "your little cat-burglar act was perhaps a little unorthodox. Bearing in mind that Major Willoughby-Styrt is, or was, a client of yours."

The Major gave a sidelong glance at Becker. "Cat-burglar?" he said.

Becker gave a pithy account of my nocturnal explorations of the Major's flat. Someone had clearly been watching me. Maybe Miss M. C. Jeevons, the occupier of the first floor flat? The Major huffed and puffed and swore a bit – but not too much, because he knew that if Becker knew all about what I'd been up to then he also knew what the Major had been up to.

"I must say," said Becker, "that I've known Edward," He glanced at the Major, "for some considerable time and yet it had never crossed my mind that he might have such proclivities."

"Proclivities!" said the Major, as though the word was unfamiliar to him.

"The Basement Club," Becker said, tonelessly. "An establishment which caters to men of a certain disposition. Don't deny it, Eddie, old man, we have the evidence. You can thank Mr Kennick for that."

For once the Major was lost for words. Becker smirked into the silence. "It really doesn't matter, however. Your private life is of no interest to us. What is of interest is the breach of security. A large number of documents have gone astray. Documents of more significance than you have confided to Mr Kennick. Those documents have been supplied by you. And where they have ended up, well, who can tell?"

"No!" The Major affected an air of humorous outrage, as though he'd been made the butt of a slightly risqué joke. "That's absurd! Me? Good Lord! I mean to say…"

Becker's face was expressionless. He stared at the Major, as though commanding silence.

"The documents relating to Turnstile are by no means as significant as they may at first appear. Turnstile is being wound down. The Government has different plans afoot."

"But, Becker, old man, you surely don't think that I…" The Major was determined to protest his innocence but his heart wasn't in it. He knew the game was up.

"Consider yourself fortunate," Becker said. "Mr Kennick has certain special talents of which we occasionally avail ourselves. Had the documents been of greater import, had we been unable to find some less disagreeable way of resolving this matter…" He trailed off, leaving the Major to draw his own conclusions.

The upshot of all this was that the Major was going to get off scot-free. That's the old boys' network for you. He'd be given a good dressing-down, he would probably be given a less important job in some stagnant backwater of the Home Office but his good character would remain intact. But that wasn't the end of the matter. The end of the matter was that the link in the chain would have to be broken.

Becker had a quiet word with me later on, as we were leaving the Major's flat. The person who'd been blackmailing the Major would have to be dealt with, he said. I told Becker it was too late for that. The blackmailer was Nathan Welbridge, the man who'd been killed at Bully Fen.

"That's one little detail you got wrong," Becker said. "You led us right to the chap we needed and yet you failed to make the proper inferences. An extraordinary oversight, if I might say so."

"Maybe I'm not infallible after all," I said. "If you tell me which inferences I failed to make, I'll tell you if I agree."

"It really doesn't matter whether you agree or not, old man. We have identified the person who's been engaged in – what shall we call it? – 'subversive' activities."

"Flogging secrets to the Soviets," I said. "Secrets provided by Major Teddy."

Becker smiled. He had a smile like a hungry boa constrictor that's just spotted a tethered goat. "The source of the leaked documents has not been established and, quite frankly, that is not relevant to the action that needs to be taken."

"You want someone removed?" I said. "Then you'd better tell me who."

*

Becker gave me a folder. I didn't open the folder until I got back to my flat. It contained all the details about my target: photo, address, height, colour of hair, a brief biography. He looked harmless enough. There was nothing in his biography to suggest that he wasn't an ordinary lad who liked to go for a few drinks and had got into a few scrapes but who was not much different from millions of other ordinary lads.

But he wasn't an ordinary lad. He had got involved in a very dangerous game. Two very dangerous games: blackmail and treason. He had blackmailed the Major to obtain certain documents and he had committed treason by selling those documents to people who did not have Britain's best interests at heart. That sort of thing happened from time to time. Usually it was dealt with quietly, efficiently and anonymously. Occasionally, news leaked out. The Government didn't like that.

The last thing the Government and the Security Services wanted was another Vassall affair. John Vassall, a junior civil servant in the Admiralty, had been supplying the Soviets with details of our naval secrets. In return the Soviets kept quiet about Vassall's secret life. But secrets have a way of getting out. When Vassall's secret got out, it made headlines in all the newspapers. Vassall was a homosexual. Blackmailers love a good homosexual scandal. So do newspaper editors.

If Becker had handled the Vassall affair, it might have all ended differently. Vassall would have had an unfortunate accident. The Great British public would never have heard the man's name. I stared at the photo in my hand. He was the sort of person you'd pass in the street without giving a second glance. And yet, according to Becker, he was an enemy of the state.

"Deal with him," Becker had told me. He knew I would. It's what I'm good at.

40. Suck It And See

Friday morning. I should have been in a good mood. It was the last day of the working week. A whole weekend full of nothing to do stretched out in front of me. But I wasn't in a good mood. I wasn't in a bad mood either. I was in a mood that could have tipped in either direction, depending on how things went. I was thinking about the job I had to do that evening. If all went well, I'd be able to spend the weekend relaxing. If all didn't go well, I'd have to make other plans. I noticed that Meek was staring at me.

"What?" I said.

"Eh?"

"You are staring at me," I said.

Meek was sitting at the other side of my desk. He'd been sitting there all morning, ever since he'd arrived which was some time after eleven. He was passing the time by folding up unpaid bills and making them into paper aeroplanes.

"I wasn't staring at you," Meek said. "I was staring at *that*."

"That?"

The kettle was whistling. I got up, spooned some tea into the pot and poured on some hot water.

"What's 'that' exactly?"

I gave the tea a stir or two then poured it into two nearly-clean mugs and sploshed in some milk from the bottle. I put a teaspoon of sugar from the open packet that I keep on the window ledge into one of the mugs. Meek likes two spoons of sugar but I'm economising and he's putting on weight, so one's the limit.

"Got any biscuits?" he said, as I handed him the mug.

I shook my head, took a good slurp from my own mug – no sugar for me; I'm putting on even more weight than Meek is.

"I was wondering. That Baron bloke. He's smuggling LSD inside knickknacks?"

I scooped Straker off my chair and sat in it. Straker leapt back up again and settled on my lap, digging in a few claws just for good measure.

"It's a possibility," I said.

"Well, do you think there might be, you know…?" He nodded towards the hideous little shepherdess statuette standing on my desk. The chances that it contained illicit drugs struck me as remote.

"Could be," I said. "I mean, where'd you say you bought it?"

"Petticoat Lane."

"How much did you pay?"

"Ten and six."

I sucked through my teeth to show that I was giving the matter long and serious thought. "Whoever sold it to you must have known that there was more to it than meets the eye."

"How do you mean?"

"Well, you have to be honest. That statuette looks like it's worth threepence-halfpenny. So I reckon the bloke who sold it to you must have thought you were in on the game."

"The game?"

"Part of the ring."

"Drug smuggling?"

"A pusher."

"So anyway," said Meek. "I was wondering. D'you think I should have a look? Inside, I mean?"

"How do you propose to do that?"

Meek stood up, went over to the sink and opened the cupboard door beneath it. I keep various cleaning things and a few essential tools down there in case I need to tighten the tap-washers or hammer in a nail to hang a calendar on the wall, that kind of thing. When Meek stood up again I saw he was holding the hammer.

With the first smash of hammer on chalk, the little shepherdess flew into pieces. Straker leapt off my lap with a startled miaow. Meek hooted with laughter.

"What are you laughing at?" I said.

"I never did like that bloody statue."

"You said you did."

"I changed my mind."

I noticed a little piece of paper lying in the chalk dust. It must have been inside the statuette. Meek picked it up.

"What is it?" I said.

"It's a ticket. A bus ticket, I think."

"Where does it go to?"

"I don't know. The writing's in Chinese."

We both stared at the ticket for a while. Then Meek said, "You think it's LSD?"

"Only one way to find out," I said. "Suck it and see."

He did.

It wasn't.

For want of anything better to do, we carried on hammering the fragments of the shepherdess to smithereens. I was in that kind of mood. I often am in that kind of mood just before the sort of job I was going to do that evening. It's a sort of suppressed hysteria, I think. Destroying that horrible statuette seemed the funniest thing I'd ever done in my life and pretty soon, Meek and I were laughing like loons. I gave a big piece of the statuette (the lamb, I think) an almighty thump and clouds of chalk dust puffed up into the air. It was just then that the doorbell tinkled and in walked a tall, serious-looking man wearing a dark suit and a bowler hat. Meek and I stared at him through the billowing clouds.

"I beg your pardon," the man said. "I was under the impression that this was the office of a private investigator."

I straightened up, brushed the chalk dust off my jacket, put the hammer carefully down upon my desk and replied, in as serious a tone as I could muster. "Kennick Investigations. How may I help you?"

But the man had already gone.

"Probably my only customer this month," I said. "And we scared him off."

But I wasn't worried about that. I'd had a chat with Becker about the remuneration for the job he wanted me to do. I'd be able to pay the bills. Maybe there'd even be enough left over to get Sol to run me up another suit. On the whole, I didn't have any cause for complaint.

41. In Cold Blood

Hanging around in a street again. It was a dingy little street down the East End. It had the stink of fried onions, dog shit and desperation. It was a warm evening and the pub at the end of the street was doing good trade; people were standing around drinking and talking on the pavement; through the open door came the sound of a piano and tuneless singing. It's what passes for entertainment in that part of town.

I was watching a small, shabby terraced house with a peeling green front door and a cardboard sign hanging in the front window: "Room To Let. Suit Single Gent. No Blacks. No Irish."

I'd been told he usually went to the pub at nine o'clock on a Friday night. I'd arrived at half past eight. I'd positioned myself further down the street, just behind a phone box. I didn't have to worry that queues might form there. The phone box didn't contain a phone. It looked as though someone had disconnected it with a pair of bolt cutters.

At ten to nine the peeling green front door of the shabby terraced house opened and a man came out. He was a young man, smartly dressed in a dark, single breasted jacket over a pale yellow roll-neck sweater, dark trousers, suede shoes, his hair light brown and wavy. He looked the sort of lad any parent would be proud of. He didn't look the sort of lad who would kill someone in cold blood.

Appearances can be deceptive.

He went down the street and into the pub. I followed. The pub was crowded. It was a typical East End pub. Most of the customers were in their fifties or sixties. There was a small group of younger people by the bar. He headed straight for them, chatted to a couple of girls and a couple of lads, then out came his wallet and he was buying drinks. Flashing his money around.

I went to the other end of the bar and ordered a pint. I had a feeling he wouldn't be staying long. When he left, so would I. I drank my beer slowly. A woman pushed past me. "Haven't seen you here before," she said. She was in her early forties, I suppose, but was doing her best to look younger. She smelled strongly of hairspray and cheap perfume. I didn't reply. I smiled. "You looking for some fun?" she said. She wasn't just making conversation. She was touting for business. "Not tonight," I said. She sighed. "Oh well, suit yourself."

When I looked towards the other end of the bar, he wasn't there. For a second, I thought he had left. Then I spotted him. He was feeding coins into the jukebox. The piano-player was having a break. So was the singer. After a few seconds, there was the sound of a record needle scratchily circling around on a disc and then came the noise of drums and an electric guitar. "Wild thing…" someone sang. Whoever it was it wasn't Frank Sinatra.

Having got the jukebox going, he went back to his friends at the bar. Someone had got another round in. It seemed he was planning to stay longer than I'd expected. I sipped my beer slowly. If I was to do the job, I had to get him alone. I was starting to think I'd have to come back some other night.

Then my luck changed. An argument broke out between him and one of the other men in the group of youngsters. One of the girls was trying to calm them down. To no avail. The man I was following pushed his way through the people standing around in the pub and left. I left too. I hung back and watched him striding away down the street. Then the door of the pub opened again and the girl who'd tried to stop the argument came out. I got the impression that she might have been the cause of the argument. With lads that age, girls often are. She was slim and good-looking; she was wearing a dress that was too short and too tight, and stiletto heels that were too high. If it hadn't been for the heels, she'd have been able to run after him. Due to the heels, the best she could do was totter like a trainee stilt-walker.

He heard the heels tapping on the pavement. He looked round and smiled. She had her coat draped over an arm. She caught up with him and he helped her put the coat on. It was a knee-length overcoat in a brilliant shade of tangerine. He smiled at her and kissed her. Then they strolled off, arm in arm. I strolled off after them, at a discreet distance. They stopped in a dark doorway. He took her in his arms and kissed her. They talked for a while. I couldn't hear what they said. She laughed. They walked on further down the street, taking a sharp left, and then the houses suddenly came to an end.

They were standing next to a rough patch of waste ground strewn with rubble. To the right of the waste ground was the wall of a house. To the left of the waste ground was the wall of another house. The waste ground itself formed a rough, rocky rectangle where five or six houses would once have stood. It was an old bombsite. Left derelict for the last twenty-five years or so. It's the sort of place that is used, by day, as a kids' playground and, by night, as a place where courting couples go. To do their courting.

I didn't want to intrude so I stayed at the end of the street. It was dark by then and I couldn't see what they were up to. Not that I cared. I needed to bide my time. I needed to get him alone. The fact that they'd gone to a patch of waste ground told me that they didn't have anywhere more comfortable to go. He was renting a room. I guessed his landlord or landlady had strict rules against lodgers bringing girls back to their rooms. And where did the girl live? At home, maybe, with her mum and dad?

Five minutes later I saw a glimmer of light – a match flame; then two red dots moving through the darkness – the glowing ends of their cigarettes. He was obviously a quick worker. Didn't bother much with romantic patter. Knickers down, a bit of how's-yer-father, then time for a quick smoke.

A few minutes later, I heard the girl say "Nighty-night, Tommy. See you tomorrow, 'ey?"

"Night, Sylvie," came the reply. "Yeah. See you."

Who was Sylvie, I wondered? What were they planning for tomorrow? I blanked that out of my mind. It was none of my business. Irrelevant to the job at hand. I've heard it's the same with surgeons. When they have to focus on the job at hand they don't see a person, they see a body, the place they have to cut, the job they have to do. If they saw a real person with a frumpy little wife, a three piece-suite on hire purchase, two kids, a dog and a one-legged budgie, they wouldn't be able to do a good job.

"Got a light, mate?" I don't smoke but I had to have some way to break the ice and that seemed as good as any. I could barely even see him at the time. He was still a couple of yards away on the bombsite whereas I was standing on the pavement. I could see the red dot of his cigarette though. It glowed brighter as he sucked in the smoke then grew dimmer as he lowered his hand to waist height.

"And who are you, then?" He had a pleasant voice and his accent was only mild, softened no doubt by the years he'd spent in the Army and then, afterwards, working in London. There was no mistaking the Welsh lilt, though. He came out of the darkness of the bombsite and into a dim pool of light from a nearby streetlamp.

"Hello, Tommy," I said.

"I asked you who you are," he said.

"I'm just someone who wants to ask you a few questions."

"Get stuffed." He pushed past me. A stupid thing to do. I grabbed him by the arm and spun him around so that he was facing me.

"No need to be rude," I said.

He looked me up and down and spoke in a monotone half-whisper. He probably thought that made him sound tough. "Get out of my way, old man." I've known plenty of tough blokes. Really tough blokes don't go in for the theatricals. They smile. They are polite. And then they break your arm. Or your neck.

"Why did you kill him?" I said.

"What? What you on about?"

"Welbridge. Nathan Welbridge. Sometimes known as Nate. Sometimes known as Corporal Welbridge."

That stopped him in his tracks. The tough expression melted away like ice in the sun. When he spoke next, there was a tremble in his voice. "I don't know what you're on about."

"Yes, Tommy, you do. I was there. Sunday, the twenty-fourth of July. Bully Fen. You and Nathan Welbridge were playing at soldiers. Carrying around people playing at being wounded, on stretchers."

"I don't know nothing about…"

"So I'm asking you again, nice and politely. Why did you kill Nathan Welbridge?

"Kill him? You're nuts, that's what you are. I didn't kill Nate. We was mates, me and him."

"Did he find out what you were up to? Blackmail. Extortion. Consorting with the enemy."

"Me? You're dead wrong there. Dead wrong."

"What happened? Were you both in on it? Did you have an argument? I heard you arguing in the pub. You've got a temper on you, haven't you."

"I didn't kill Nate."

"Or was he in on the job too? Maybe he was getting too greedy? Too much of a risk."

"Fuck's sake! I didn't kill him."

He didn't look like a killer. But who does? Becker had been tracking him. He hadn't told me the whole story because, as far as Becker was concerned, I didn't need to know. But I guessed that this lad, Tommy Evans, had been blackmailing the Major. The Major had pilfered some documents and given them to Evans. Then Evans had sold them on to…. Who? The Russians? The Spies For Peace or some other ban-the-bomb fanatics? My guess was the Russians. But Becker was right – I didn't need to know.

"I don't know who put you onto me, mate." He was shaking visibly now. I could hear the quaver in his voice. "But whatever they told you, they told you wrong. I never got involved in none of that stuff."

"What stuff?"

He hesitated. He wasn't sure how much I knew. He couldn't decide how much he should say. I was hoping he'd calm down. I was hoping he would see reason. There was still a chance that we could sort this all out. I had no grouse against the lad. I knew next to nothing about him. If only he could get himself under control and not do anything stupid…

Some hope!

"Piss off!" he said.

"That's not a good attitude, son. I just want you to tell me who you've been dealing with."

"I don't know what you are on about, mate. And even if I did, I wouldn't tell you."

"I think you should."

"Oh, yeah? And who's gonna make me? You?"

"Yes."

He laughed. His confidence was coming back, powered up by the adrenaline pumping through his veins. He was a hard man again. In his prime. He looked at me and he saw a middle-aged man, not as fit as he should be, someone gone soft, a pushover. That's where he made a mistake.

"Just tell me why you killed him," I said.

"Get out of my fucking…"

It was then that I saw the knife. It had been in a pocket of his jacket. He'd pulled it out while we'd been having our little chat. It wasn't a Fairbairn-Sykes. In fact, it wasn't a fighting knife at all. It was a flick-knife. One of those cheap and nasty little knives that is nothing but a handle until you press a button when out pops the blade. It's not what I'd call a serious knife. Oh, it can do serious damage all right, if the person wielding it knows how to handle a knife in a fight and the person at the other end of the blade doesn't. But Taffy didn't know how to handle it. He was waggling the bloody thing, point first, in my face. That was intended to terrify me. It didn't have the desired effect.

"You silly bloody bugger," I said. "Put the knife away. Just tell me what I want to know and…"

I couldn't think how to finish the sentence but I didn't have to bother because in the next second he came for me, slashing the air with that damned silly knife. Slashing away like that looks impressive – if you don't understand knife-fighting – but it's the stupidest thing you can do. For every forward slash you have to take a backward slash to get your hand in the starting position for the next forward slash. The forward slash is dangerous. The backward slash just takes up time. Which gave me the advantage. He took a backward slash. I saw my opportunity. Using my left arm, thrust out straight, I blocked his forearm so he couldn't complete the forward slash. Immediately, I gripped his hand, the hand that was holding the knife, in my right hand. So now I was holding his knife through his hand. In that moment, he was disarmed. I was in control. I twisted his wrist back so that the tip of his knife was pointing back towards him. All it took then was a single thrust and it was all over. The poor kid didn't know what was happening. His eyes went wide, he made a grunting noise as though I'd punched him in the solar plexus. Then he slumped against the wall and collapsed. He was dead before he hit the ground.

42. Unfinished Business

"What the fuck happened to you?"

It was Monday morning. I was struggling to make the tea one-handed. My left hand was bandaged. The stitches in my forearm were aching like the blazes.

"I had a bit of a run-in with a man and a knife," I said.

Meek laughed. "Tell me."

I told him. He laughed even louder. Meek has a lively sense of humour when it comes to someone else's pain. The funny thing is, I don't remember being cut. All I remember is Tommy Evans taking a swing at me with his knife, me blocking with my arm, and him grunting as the knife went in. That's the way knife fights are. Years ago, my unarmed combat instructor used to say that you should go into a knife fight knowing you will be cut. Only by accepting that fact will you be able to keep your head. Which is great advice. Until you are actually in a knife fight. Because when you are in a knife fight everything happens so damn' fast that you haven't got time to think about anything except staying alive.

"So what was his game, then, this Taffy bloke?"

I'd told Meek everything I knew about Taffy Evans. I'd told him everything I knew about Nathan Welbridge and Major Edward Willoughby-Styrt and the whole damn' business. Becker wouldn't have liked it if he knew I'd told Meek. McJay wouldn't have liked it either. Too bad. I trusted Meek. I didn't trust Becker and McJay.

"I suppose," said Meek, "the Welsh git had been blackmailing Major Teddy? Flogging our bog roll secrets to the Russians? And then, what happened? He was in cahoots with Nathan Welbridge. But they fell out. So Taffy bumped him off?" Meek was enjoying himself. I'd bought in some Garibaldi biscuits. He was dunking them into his tea and chuckling to himself. "A neat little swindle, I'd say. Dangerous though."

"The only thing is…." I said.

"What?"

"I don't think he did it."

"Who?"

"Tommy Evans. Taffy."

"What? You don't reckon he was flogging secrets to the Ruskies?"

"I don't think he killed Nathan Welbridge."

"Give over! 'Course he did."

"He didn't know how to handle a knife. He was a novice. He had no idea."

Meek drank some tea and stroked the cat who happened to be sleeping on Meek's lap at the time. When you do this kind of job, you want it to have a neat ending. A satisfactory resolution. This one didn't. I knew it didn't. Meek knew it didn't. There was no point worrying about that, though. What's done was done. It wasn't my problem.

So we talked about the weather a bit and Meek told me some cock-and-bull story about a mate of his who was smuggling diamonds in a one-legged stripper's wooden leg. I tried not to laugh. I didn't have to try very hard. Meek didn't hang around long after that. He said he had some "important business" in Wapping. I didn't ask for details. When Meek went out, so did the cat. Maybe the cat had some important business too. Which just left me. I sat at my desk, drank my tea and shuffled through a small pile of post: a couple of bills, a final demand from the electricity board, a leaflet from the Jehovah's Witnesses. I needed a client. A nice, easy, run-of-the-mill job. Another light-fingered florist would have been ideal. Nothing too demanding. Just something to take my mind off things.

I picked up the phone. There was a certain person I wanted to speak to. I had to go through the usual palaver. The person who answered the phone wanted to know my name and "the nature of my enquiry", tried to fob me off, pretended he wasn't there, that I'd got the wrong number, blah-de-blah-de-blah. I don't like swearing on the phone but sometimes there are no options. Eventually I got put through.

"Ah, Mr Kennick! I was about to phone you."

McJay could barely open his mouth without telling a lie so I paid no attention.

"I asked to talk to Becker," I said.

"Mr Becker is not available, I'm afraid. I, however, am fully at your disposal. How may I help?"

"I want to know what it was all about."

"I beg your…"

"Don't piss me about. You set me up. I could have been killed."

He sniggered. "Oh, really, I don't think there was ever any danger of that."

"You're right. There wasn't."

"Quite so."

"Because he was the wrong man."

"I beg your…"

I gave him my theory about who the right man was. I added a few ideas I'd had about why they were covering things up and why an innocent man had to die in order to do so.

McJay interrupted me. "Most fanciful, Mr Kennick. If it is any consolation, I may put your mind at rest, the evidence against Thomas Jones…"

"Evans!" I said. McJay couldn't even be bothered to get his name right!

"Ah yes, quite. The evidence against him is quite overwhelming. The police searched his lodgings, you see. In so doing, they discovered a number of, well, compromising documents. They handed them over to us, naturally. Since they are not the sort of documents which are intended for public viewing."

"The stolen documents?"

"So it would seem."

I'd had enough. I called McJay a few names that I'd learnt in the Army but hadn't had much occasion to use ever since. Then I added, "An innocent man died all because you wanted to protect your own."

There was a pause on the line. When McJay spoke next, his voice had a serious tone which I had rarely heard from him before. "He was not innocent. Of that I can assure you."

"What exactly do you mean by…?"

"My dear fellow!" The oily, devil-may-care tone was back in his voice now. "You must know that there are certain things which I am not at liberty to…"

"Yeah, yeah, yeah...." I put the phone down. I couldn't bear to listen to him a moment longer.

At half-past twelve, I shut up the office. I decided to go back to my flat and have a lazy afternoon, listen to music, read a book. I dawdled. There is nothing about my flat that makes me want to get there quickly. It was a typical August day in suburbia. The sky was grey, the birds weren't singing, a warm breeze blew the litter decoratively over the pavement. I went into a shop and bought a strawberry ice-lolly. I was sucking the dreg-ends of the lolly as I turned into the street where I live. It's a shabby street lined with shabby houses. I blend in perfectly. As I was going down the street, a red Jaguar drove past. The driver was a youngish man, very fashionably dressed. He slowed down, tooted the horn and waved. I didn't wave back. It could have been pure chance that Simon Baron happened to be taking a quiet drive through my house on a gloomy Monday afternoon, but I didn't think so. I had an uncomfortable feeling that, where he and I were concerned, there was still some unfinished business. One day I would have to finish it.

PostScript: How Much Of This Is True?

The Civil Defence exercises in Bully Fen, the network of ROC observation posts and bunkers, the wardens and maroons that would alert the British public when the bomb dropped, Turnstile (by that and its other names), The Spies For Peace and their pamphlet 'Danger! Official Secret', and many other details relating to Britain's preparations for a nuclear attack, are all true. The principal characters and events in this novel, however, are fictitious.

Printed in Great Britain
by Amazon

47573862R00121